## "You Know, Vanessa," Brock Said, "I Was In A Devil Of A Mood When I Got Here...."

"Ready to take my head off?" she asked nervously.

"Well, I'm definitely ready to take *something* off," he said quietly.

She remained silent. Even as he set his glass down on the counter. Even as he walked toward her. Even as he stood toe to toe with her, backing her against the granite countertop.

"My mood *is* improving," he said, touching a strand of her hair and looking down at her mouth.

Her heart raced. She didn't know what to do. She'd spent the day sabotaging his [illegible]ess, but now, as he bent his head, s[illegible] [illegible]el his lips claim hers again[illegible] swept through her.

"This is cra[illegible]

"Why?" he a[illegible]od scent surrounding h[illegible]

*Because I'm do[illegible] my best to ruin you....*

Dear Reader,

I've never met a tropical island I didn't like! Maui is one of my favorites, with its stunning golden sunsets and deep aqua blue waters. So it seemed fitting that the final SUITE SECRETS story, *Reserved for the Tycoon,* would conclude where it began initially with *The Corporate Raider's Revenge,* in Hawaii.

I've always wanted to write a story filled with deception in its simplest form. With Brock Tyler and Vanessa Dupree you'll meet two people who are as cunning as they are appealing. I enjoyed plotting their escapades, where nothing is as it seems and their cagey games of cat and mouse end only when they enter the bedroom. There, the sizzling heat of the tropics is turned up and emotions run very high.

Make your reservation to be swept away with surprising twists and turns and of course, romance.

"Suite" Reading!

*Charlene*

# RESERVED FOR THE TYCOON

CHARLENE SANDS

Published by Silhouette Books
**America's Publisher of Contemporary Romance**

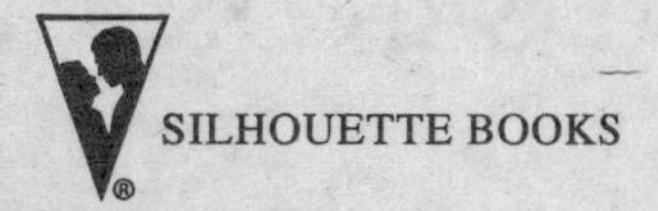

Recycling programs for this product may not exist in your area.

ISBN-13: 978-0-373-76924-7
ISBN-10: 0-373-76924-5

RESERVED FOR THE TYCOON



This edition published by arrangement with Harlequin Books S.A.



Visit Silhouette Books at www.eHarlequin.com

**Printed in U.S.A.**

**Books by Charlene Sands**

Silhouette Desire

*The Heart of a Cowboy* #1488
*Expecting the Cowboy's Baby* #1522
*Like Lightning* #1668
*Heiress Beware* #1729
*Bunking Down with the Boss* #1746
*Fortune's Vengeful Groom* #1783
*Between the CEO's Sheets* #1805
*Five-Star Cowboy* #1889
*Do Not Disturb Until Christmas* #1906
*Reserved for the Tycoon* #1924

Harlequin Historical

*Lily Gets Her Man* #554
*Chase Wheeler's Woman* #610
*The Law and Kate Malone* #646
*Winning Jenna's Heart* #662
*The Courting of Widow Shaw* #710
*Renegade Wife* #789
*Abducted at the Altar* #816

---

## *CHARLENE SANDS*

resides in Southern California with her husband, high school sweetheart and best friend, Don. Proudly, they boast that their children, Jason and Nikki, have earned their college degrees. The "empty nesters" now have two cats that have taken over the house.

Charlene has written twenty-five romances and is the recipient of the 2008 Booksellers' Best Award, the 2007 Cataromance Reviwer's Choice Award and the 2006 National Readers' Choice Award. When not writing, she enjoys sunny California days, Pacific beaches and sitting down with a good book.

She blogs regularly on the all-western site www.petticoatsandpistols.com, and you can also find her at www.myspace.com/charlenesands.

Charlene invites you to visit her Web site at www.charlenesands.com to enter her contests and see what's new.

To my dear mother-in-law Nancy,
whose support and love mean a great deal to me.
You are very close to my heart.

# One

Getting the job at Tempest Maui Hotel as event planner had been a breeze. With her impressive résumé in hand, Vanessa Dupree walked right into today's interview with confidence and answered the hotel tycoon's questions with all of the intelligence and charm she possessed. Then she smiled winningly with promise in her eyes. Promises that arched Brock Tyler's dark eyebrows a bit and had his gaze wandering to her "other" assets.

Vanessa silently fumed. Brock was a charmer, all right. Black hair, perfectly groomed, dark eyes that could mesmerize and classy clothes covering a fit body; it was a small wonder her younger sister fell for him back in New Orleans.

He didn't know that Melody Applegate and Vanessa Dupree were related and that's exactly how she intended on keeping it. Vanessa shoved the image of her heartbroken sister, teary-eyed and devastated, out of her mind, for now.

She rose from her seat. "Thank you for the opportunity, Mr. Tyler. You won't be sorry you hired me."

The lie flowed easily from her lips.

He stood up and instead of reaching across his desk for a handshake, walked around to grasp her hand and give a gentle but firm tug. "The success of this hotel is very important to me. I handpick all my employees. Welcome to the team, Miss Dupree."

Vanessa squirmed a little under his steady gaze. He stood a head taller than her and she felt his dominating presence far more than when a bamboo-accented desk separated them. The man oozed sexual prowess with every movement he made and his hand touching hers brought queasy jitters to her stomach. "Thank you."

"I'll see you tonight for dinner."

"Dinner?" Vanessa's voice squeaked. The man worked fast.

"There's an employee dinner meeting every Wednesday night. Seven o'clock in the Aloha conference room."

"Right," she said, steadying her nerves. "I'll be there."

Brock nodded and walked her to the door, his eyes

flickering from her tightly pulled back platinum hair, down the bodice of her navy-blue business suit, lingering a second on her breasts, then to the hem of her dress. "We dress more casual here. We want the guests to feel relaxed. No more business suits and…let your hair down."

Sizzling heat rivaling the Hawaiian sun raced through her system when his gaze returned to her hair. She touched a strand absently. "It's natural. The color, I mean."

*Good heavens, Vanessa. Get a grip.*

Those dark brows rose again, but he didn't voice his doubt.

"My mother always said it was a freak of nature. No one in the family has this color hair."

He looked at her hair again and nodded. "Pretty."

"Oh, I wasn't fishing for a compliment, Mr. Tyler."

Though that's exactly how she'd sounded.

"No, I doubt you'd have to hunt down compliments, *Vanessa.*"

The soft tone of his voice when he spoke her name brought another round of jitters to her stomach.

He was good, she surmised.

Sexy. Rich. Powerful.

But Vanessa wouldn't let that discourage her from her mission. She thought of the pain he'd caused Melody last month. Her sister had been beside herself with grief. She'd fallen hard and fast for her tycoon employer in New Orleans and Brock had discarded her like yesterday's newspaper. To him, she was old news. Vanessa had never seen her sister cry so much or so hard. She'd been destroyed by his abrupt dismissal and rejection. He hadn't cared that he'd broken her young naive heart after dating her for weeks and leading her on.

Vanessa had firsthand experience with this kind of man. She'd been dumped a few times and she remembered how much that had hurt. She learned how to weed out the insincere men and steer clear. Melody, on the other hand, being six years her junior, hadn't the experience to handle a man like Brock Tyler.

Vanessa had always championed her younger half sister's cause. She'd watched out for her. She'd protected her all of her life. In most respects, she'd mothered Melody when their own mother had become too ill to do it. Vanessa had taken over the role then and those tendencies were hard to change.

Compelled by anger and a sense of justice, Vanessa couldn't pass up this chance to finally give Brock Tyler a taste of his own medicine. The event planner position had fallen into her lap. She'd always wanted to see Hawaii, and now she'd be here for a time, subletting a little condo on the island. All things had fallen into place.

Yet, after meeting Brock Tyler, Vanessa understood the challenge. It wouldn't be easy. He'd be a worthy adversary but that wouldn't deter her. She'd come to the island for one reason and one reason only.

To ruin Brock Tyler.

* * *

"Vanessa Dupree is teaching the class?" Brock Tyler watched his new event planner on an exercise mat lift one firm, gorgeous leg over her head on Tempest Maui's sandy beachfront.

"Yes, sir." Akamu Ho, his hotel manager, nodded. "Pilates. She didn't want our guests to miss out when Lucy called in sick this morning."

"Enterprising woman." His newest employee had spunk and a great résumé. From the moment they'd met in the interview, Brock had been intrigued. He'd debated about hiring her. His instant attraction to her had knocked his well-honed senses off the charts. Not that Brock had trouble mixing business with pleasure normally, but he couldn't jeopardize the success of Tempest Maui. His focus and all of his attention had to be directed to the newly renovated hotel.

Brock walked from the plush Garden Pavilion onto the sands of Tranquility Bay toward the dozen guests working out on the beach. When Vanessa spotted him, she wiggled three fingers in a wave.

Her natural smile and that Marilyn Monroe hair were eye-stopping enough, but add the skimpy black spandex shorts with her tanned midriff exposed and Brock had a helluva time containing his lust.

He leaned against a tall palm tree and waited for her to finish. After leading the class in a cooldown exercise that had his blood heating up, she dismissed the class. He walked over to her, helping her pick up the mats and stack them in one pile on the sand. "So you're a Pilates expert, too? I didn't see that in your résumé."

Her low rumble of throaty laughter brought images of hot sex on the sand. "I'm not an expert. I just enjoy exercise. I've always been flexible."

Brock cleared his throat, but that image of sex with her on the sand went from hazy to vivid in two seconds flat.

"When Lucy called in sick with a high fever, I didn't want to disappoint the guests. I let them know I wasn't an expert or anything, but I could lead them in a class."

She picked up a towel and wiped sweat from her forehead. Beads of perspiration coated her body and brought a shimmering sheen to her tanned skin.

"They all thanked me," she said with a slight shrug. "I think they enjoyed it."

"I'm sure they did," Brock said, trying to keep his mind on the reason he'd come out here. "In just the week you've worked here, you've made an impression. Stepping in today for Lucy shows you've got team spirit and the hotel's interests in mind."

With the towel placed around her neck, she gazed into his eyes, squinting a bit in the sunlight. "Are you saying you're glad you hired me?"

She surprised him with her blunt assessment. "I'm a good judge of character."

Then he focused on the reason for approaching her in the first place, setting aside the fact that he'd have watched her do her *flexible* exercises for no other reason than pure fascination. "Actually, I need to speak with you about some upcoming events that are important to the hotel."

"Okay. Should I shower and change and meet you in your office?"

That had been his plan initially, but now it seemed sacrilegious to ask a gorgeous woman to change out of revealing spandex. "No, let's walk the beach. I've got a full schedule today and doubt I'll get outside again before the sun sets."

That much was true. Brock didn't spend enough time outside on these gorgeous Hawaiian days. Whenever he could, he'd go out on his yacht, harbored in Tranquility Bay to get away from the mounds of paperwork he'd encountered since the renovation project began months ago. Now he had a wager with his brother Trent, for ego's sake more than anything else, to make a bigger success of his hotel than Trent had with Tempest West in Arizona. The two had always been competitive and with the added bonus of his late father's beloved classic Thunderbird as the prize, Brock had everything to gain by seeing that his hotel prospered.

They walked in morning sunshine along the warm sand, the ocean humming more like a small kitten than a lion's roar.

Brock got right to the point. "These first few events will make or break our hotel's reputation. As you know, this hotel had been closed down for more than a year due to poor management. Certainly not because of location. My brothers and I saw the hotel's great potential as a destination spot for weddings, conventions, fashions shows and major parties. The renovations are complete and now it's up to all of us, including you, to see that we succeed, Vanessa."

Vanessa nodded, her head down. "I understand that, sir."

He winced at her serious tone. He was used to commanding respect from his employees, but somehow, the "sir" coming from Vanessa's sensual lips didn't sound quite right. "Call me Brock."

When she glanced up, he smiled. "We'll be working closely from now on. You and I might as well drop the formalities."

"Okay...Brock." She cast him a quick coy smile.

Brock couldn't quite figure her out. Several times this week he'd caught her watching him, but the minute their eyes met she'd looked away abruptly. What had he witnessed in those pretty blue eyes?

"We have a wedding next week. It's a big expensive affair and the hotel has booked over three hundred guests. You've been working with the wedding coordinator, I suspect?"

"Yes, since the moment I hired on. I have the details covered, Mr....uh, Brock."

"Good."

"I've done wedding coordinating before. I've got it under control."

Her qualifications were impeccable. She'd had experience in event planning for a large corporation as well as a major hotel chain, working at one time for a competitor, actually. Brock had been fortunate she'd come along when she had.

"I'm counting on your expertise to make this happen."

"I'm good at making things…*happen.*" She spoke that last word softly, the woman oozing sensuality.

Brock stopped to gaze into her eyes. A little, throaty laugh escaped and he didn't mistake the demure look she cast him. "How good?" he asked, all thought of business now out of his mind.

"Oh, very good," she whispered, her gaze dropping to his mouth.

Brock was ready to pull her into his arms and crush his lips to hers, until she took a step back. "About the other events?"

"We'll talk about those later," he said, keeping his frustration at bay. He'd almost kissed her. Hell, he wanted to, but she'd backed off.

"Is there anything else you'd like to discuss with me?"

He shook his head. "No. Just concentrate on the wedding."

"Okay. Well, I'd better get to that shower now. I have work to do." She turned and jogged away, leaving him a stunning view of her backside and wondering what she'd do if he'd joined her in the shower.

* * *

Vanessa drove her MINI Cooper to Lucy's small home in a residential part of the island. She parked her car and carefully juggled a pot of homemade chicken soup and a bag of navel oranges. Knocking had been tricky, but she managed and waited for Lucy to open the door.

"Hi. Did I catch you napping?"

Lucy looked miserable. Her long raven hair was disheveled and her eyes were watery. "No, I'm up. Are you sure you want to come in? I don't know what I have, but it's nasty."

"I'm sure. Don't worry, I never get sick. I brought you the cure. Hot chicken soup and fresh-squeezed orange juice. I'm the squeezer," she added, chuckling.

Lucy opened the door wider and Vanessa entered. "You're so sweet to do this, but remember I warned you."

"I'll take my chances."

Lucy shook her head and sighed. "You fill in for me today with my class and now you bring me nourishment. How can I ever thank you?"

"You can tell me where can I put these things."

"Oh, follow me."

They walked into a big kitchen area, which seemed to also serve as her main living space, an oblong bay window caught a view of the Pacific Ocean between rooftops. Vanessa set the bag of oranges on the bright-white-tiled countertop and handed Lucy the soup container. "This place is great."

"Thanks," she said, her eyes sparking with pride as she set the soup pot onto a four-burner range. "It's small and affordable and I couldn't resist the view. Any place here with a view goes for a bundle, so I consider myself lucky."

"How are you feeling?"

"My fever's gone. Now I'm just exhausted." Lucy plopped into a dark cane chair and gestured for Vanessa to also sit at the kitchen table.

Vanessa shook her head. "No, let me heat up the soup and squeeze you some juice. I'll have it all ready in no time."

"This is very nice of you," Lucy said.

"You were friendly to me all week at the hotel and I...well, I don't have any friends on the island yet. Besides, I'm kind of a nurturer. My younger sister would say too much so. Just kick me out when you want to rest."

"Fair deal."

Vanessa turned the knob on the gas range to simmer then found a knife from a block on the counter. "Do you have a juicer?"

"Just a manual one in that drawer behind you."

Vanessa found the juicer and began twisting cut oranges onto the cone-shaped device.

"So how did the class go?"

"You mean after I told the disappointed guests that you were out sick? I guess it went okay. Not too many grumbles," Vanessa said, smiling while pressing half an orange down, squeezing out every last ounce of juice. "I didn't expect the big boss to show up."

"Mr. Tyler was there?" Lucy's expression brightened.

"Yep. He watched me through the class, probably making sure I didn't scare any guests away."

"He's dedicated to the hotel," Lucy said, dreamy-eyed. "He's got some sort of competition going with his brother. He told the staff about it when we all hired on. Big bonuses for all of us if the hotel does well."

Vanessa couldn't conceal a frown. "Is that so?"

He'd brought devastation to Melody without blinking an eye, walking out on her when she'd needed him the most. He'd abandoned her for another woman and now Vanessa couldn't wait to work on her plan to screw up the beloved Tempest Maui.

To think he'd almost kissed her today. And she'd almost allowed it to happen. She'd been drawn to those dark, promising eyes, and that killer smile could do a weaker woman in. He was attracted to her and she decided that it could only work to her advantage.

Maybe next time, she would allow him to kiss her.

"Yeah, he's been a good boss so far. He's given me free rein to run the gym the way I see fit and I appreciate his confidence in me. I think every female employee from sixteen to sixty has a major crush on him."

Vanessa's jaw dropped. "Really?"

Lucy bit her lip guiltily and nodded. So Lucy could be included in with the smitten females.

"Really," she confessed. "Aren't you slightly attracted to him?"

"Me?" Vanessa's voice elevated so much, she coughed to hide her scorn. "I hardly know him."

"You've just been here a short while. Give it time. You'll see."

"I hope not," she whispered softly.

"What?"

"Nothing. Your juice is ready," she said, pouring her a nice tall glass. "Drink up." She handed Lucy the glass and then turned to the range and stirred the soup. "I'll have you feeling better in no time."

# Two

Two days later, Vanessa tied the laces on her running shoes, did a few warm-up stretches on the sand and began jogging along the coast of Tranquility Bay. Early breezes cooled the air considerably and made her morning jog all the more pleasurable. She waved at guests she recognized on the beach, early birds like herself, who enjoyed the sunrise and came out for a walk or to sit quietly on the beach before the day erupted. She recognized a few she knew were here for the wedding taking place on Saturday afternoon and fought the guilt she felt over causing them any discomfort. This was the bride's third marriage and the groom's fourth, millionaires who had nothing better to spend their money on than an elaborate party for themselves, she rationalized.

Vanessa jogged to the south tip of the bay where a parking lot of boats were moored in the marina and seagulls squawked out of unison while perched atop buoys. Stunning blue-green waters shimmered, in great contrast with her hometown's mighty muddy waterway, the Mississippi River.

"Vanessa?" Brock's voice broke through her thoughts and she nearly stumbled when she caught sight of him in blue jeans and a white T-shirt, walking down the long wood dock, heading straight for her.

She halted, but jogged in place, waiting for him to come down the steps to join her on the path. She wished he didn't look so darn appealing—tanned and healthy, even without his millionaire attire on. "Hello." She stopped, trying not to ogle his perfect biceps.

"Good morning. Enjoying your jog?"

She was, up until a minute ago. "Yes, it's a habit of mine."

"Running?"

"It clears my head. Gets me ready for work." She'd run in half marathons for most of her adult life, she didn't add. "What brings you here?" she asked, being polite since conversation seemed to be on his mind this morning.

"I'm checking out Rebecca."

Rebecca? Of course, another woman. He probably

had one in every port. What could she say to that? "Well, I'd better be on my way."

"Rebecca's my boat," he said with a sly grin. "I named her after my mother." He pointed to the impressive yacht in the farthest slip in the marina. "She's been under repair."

Her heart melted into a puddle of warmth. His uncharacteristic gesture touched her in an elemental way. "I'm sorry to hear you lost your mother."

Brock tossed his head back and chuckled. "My mother's very much alive. Probably going to get married again soon. But I appreciate your kindness."

Vanessa blinked away her puzzlement, then felt foolish for her assumption. The man twisted her into knots. She needed an easy escape. "I've got a lot of details to go over for the Everett wedding, I'd better head back now."

"Just a sec," he said, taking her wrist gently. "Come see the boat," he said. "I could use your opinion about something."

"My opinion?" Vanessa nearly gasped. "I don't know a thing about boats."

"You're a woman. You'll have an opinion, believe me."

What choice did she have? "Okay." And just like that, Brock slipped his fingers from her wrist to her palm and guided her up the dock that way, holding her hand.

Tingles mingled with wariness, putting Vanessa on

guard. He had a firm grip, one that made a girl feel protected and safe. "Hah," she mumbled aloud.

"What?"

"Oh, it's lovely here," she said, covering her verbal blunder.

Thankfully, he didn't comment. And once they reached the end of the dock, he climbed onto the boat and turned to help her aboard. His touch brought unwelcome trembles and that knot inside twisted tighter. He released her immediately and smiled. "This is it. The *Rebecca.*"

A question entered her mind and Vanessa had to ask, "Why'd you name the boat after your mother?"

He scratched the back of his head, drew his brows together and replied almost reluctantly, "I lost a bet with my brother."

"You…" And then it hit her. Those warm feelings she'd held for him minutes ago vanished and the relief she felt brought a smile to her lips. "You lost a *bet?*"

"I know," he said, smiling, too. "Terrible, isn't it? Trent and I have ongoing bets and it usually takes my older brother Evan to referee. My mother doesn't know that, though, and it made her happy when I told her. So all was not lost. I'm used to the name, but the one I picked fit me better."

Brock's honesty seemed genuine…and human. She couldn't get caught up in that moment of sincerity, she reminded herself. "Which was?"

"Winning B.E.T."

"Catchy," she said. "Stands for Brock Elliot Tyler, right?"

"You've done your homework. I like that," he said, his dark eyes gleaming in a way that made her heart pound against her chest.

She shrugged. "It's not rocket science to know your employer's full name."

Brock frowned and cast her a piercing look. "Can we pretend I'm not your employer right now?"

*But you are,* she wanted to scream. "Um, sure."

He took her hand again and she followed him to the opposite end of the boat where a lavish table was set for two. "This is where I need your opinion. Can't decide on whether to have eggs Benedict or a veggie omelet for breakfast. Which do you prefer?"

She stared at him in disbelief. "Are you inviting me for breakfast?"

His eyes flickered to the table, then back to her and then the thought struck. "You knew I'd be running this way this morning?" She pointed toward the place where they'd first met. "And you planned this?"

He shrugged. "I've seen you run every day this week. Today I thought I'd ask you to join me for breakfast."

Vanessa was flattered and confused. "You could have called me up and asked me."

"Would you have said yes?"

She opened her mouth to respond, then clamped it shut. Self-conscious, she touched her hair and shoved the tresses that had come loose back into her ponytail. "I'm hardly dressed for—"

His gaze roamed over her gray sweatpants and tank top, appreciation evident in his eyes. "You look… *good,* Vanessa. There's no formality here, I'm in jeans."

She'd noticed. They fit him so well, hugging his waist and outlining his perfect butt. "Why?"

He scrubbed his face, running a hand down his jawline. "It's just breakfast on my boat. Are you hungry?"

"I could eat," she said, smiling at him, wiping the annoyance from her face. No sense riling the boss, at least not this way. "Thank you. I accept."

"That was hard work," he grumbled. "Are you this tough on all the men in your life?"

"There are no men in my life."

A satisfied gleam entered his dark eyes. He pulled her up against him, his hands wrapping around her waist as he leaned in, his mouth inches from hers. "I'd like to change that."

Good heavens, Brock knew how to kiss. His lips brushed hers gently, giving her a tantalizing taste of what was to come. He held her loosely at first, but as he deepened the kiss, he pulled her closer, enveloping her in his fresh, sandalwood scent. Then he released her for a moment, looking into her eyes. "I like you, Vanessa."

"One would hope, by the way you just kissed me."

Warmth sparkled in his eyes and an infectious smile widened his luscious mouth. "You're not like other women," he seemed to puzzle out loud.

"Why not? What's wrong with me?"

He took her back into his arms, crushing his lips to hers again, her willpower waning, her mission all but forgotten. "Nothing at all," he whispered.

Brock leaned in and once again Vanessa fell into his kiss, her mind checking out for a moment. She hadn't been kissed this passionately since…she couldn't recall a time when she'd been so wrapped up in a man that she'd forgotten all good sense.

Suddenly, all the other men in her life paled in comparison to Brock Tyler. For the next few moments, Vanessa enjoyed being in his arms, enjoyed the heady taste of him and his male scent blending with the salty sea breeze. She enjoyed his expert mouth and his firm tight body pressed to her.

Then reality set in.

*What's wrong with you, Vanessa? He's your nemesis, the man you came here to ruin.*

As if she'd willed it, her stomach growled and she pushed Brock away slightly, pasting on her most charming smile. "I guess I'm really hungry…for breakfast that is."

Brock inhaled a sharp breath. "Right, breakfast."

"Right," she repeated, stepping even farther from

him, "You know, the reason you hijacked me from my run."

"Got it," he said, casting her a hungry look that had nothing to do with veggie omelets. "Have a seat. I'll talk to the chef. Pour us some pineapple juice while you're waiting."

Vanessa rose from her seat the moment Brock headed inside and chastised herself for letting him get to her. She'd wanted him to kiss her, and now that she knew what it was like, she sympathized with Melody all the more.

She could see how an innocent, less experienced girl could fall victim to Brock in a heartbeat. He was smooth and charming and sexy as hell.

She fanned herself and then steadied her wayward nerves. When Brock came back, she looked cool as a cucumber, sitting at the table, sipping juice from a hundred-dollar Waterford Crystal.

A feast of food was served from the galley by the chef and Brock thanked him as way of dismissal. When he disappeared out of view, she dug into her food, ignoring the fact that she and Brock locked lips pretty hot and heavily just a few minutes ago.

"This is so good," she confessed, relishing every bite of the meal. "More than I usually eat for breakfast." She gobbled up the veggie omelet covered with mango sauce, fresh fruit and with a measure of guilt, popped a tiny pastry into her mouth then washed it down with a cup of Kona coffee. She doubted she'd be able to jog back to the hotel after this.

"I'll confess, it's more than I eat every morning, too."

She didn't doubt it. He'd never keep such a muscular physique if he ate like this every day.

"But, I will admit to having an enormous appetite." He glanced at her mouth, then leaned over and kissed her quickly. "You had some mango at the corner of your lip."

Darn he was fast and…charming. She swiped at her mouth with her napkin and looked over the rest of her body for food remnants, for fear he'd take her to bed to cleanse her of them. "You could have just told me."

He rubbed his nose, trying to hide a smile. "I like my way better."

"Do you always get your way?" she asked quietly, her question pointless. They both knew he was a man who got whatever he wanted.

He glanced at her in a knowing way, looking her over from head to toe, his gaze hot with sexual promise. "Not today, I won't."

She stared into his eyes, captivated for a moment, her breath catching in her throat. "You won't?"

"Vanessa, I don't play games. I want you, but it's too soon. C'mon," he said, rising and reaching for her hand. "I'll walk you back to the hotel."

*It was too soon?* Vanessa worked in her office through most of the day repeating Brock's words in her mind, her anger rising as each hour passed.

He wanted her, but it was too soon.

His comment meant that she hadn't a choice in the matter. Did he bother to ask if she were interested? No, he just assumed that one day, he'd get what he wanted.

Her.

His arrogance knew no bounds.

Vanessa thought of Melody and wondered if he'd given her sister fair warning. Or had he just showered her with charm and sex appeal and taken what he wanted, then dumped her for the next female challenge that had come along.

Every time she thought of Melody's heartbreak over Brock Tyler, she silently vowed to make him pay with the one thing that seemed to really matter to him—his hotel.

"Focus on that, Vanessa," she muttered, while going over the files for the Everett wedding. *And stop thinking about how Brock's lips worked magic over yours and how his strong muscular arms wrapped you up in a cocoon of safety and warmth.*

"What's the frown about?" Lucy walked into her office with a beautiful arrangement of island flowers and set them down on her desk.

"Lucy! These are beautiful. But you didn't have to—"

Lucy put up a stopping hand. "Whoa! Don't get ahead of yourself. I wish these were in my budget, but I'm afraid all I can offer for curing me is a drink or two at Joe's Tiki Torch on the beach. When Akamu saw me headed this way, he handed me the flowers and asked if I could bring them to you."

"From Akamu? Is it tradition for new employees to receive these?"

"Not that I know of," she said, narrowing her eyes. "I've never gotten flowers like these from anyone around here." She pointed. "There's a card."

Vanessa plucked the card out of the envelope, her suspicions aroused. She read it silently.

*I've never enjoyed breakfast more.*

*Brock*

Vanessa's knees went weak. Without elaborate words, the simple sweet sentiment touched her. Images replayed in her mind of Brock's calling to her from the dock, seeking her out and inviting her to breakfast. He'd said all the right things and she'd found him easy to be with, until he'd kissed her with so much passion, he stole her breath. Instant awareness sparked between them and Vanessa had had to back off. For her own sanity.

He'd known exactly how to push her buttons. He was smooth—she'd give him that. But a few kisses and gorgeous flowers wouldn't change anything.

"Well?" Lucy stood impatiently by, trying to peek at the card. "Who sent them to you?"

"Oh, uh," she stumbled and hated fibbing to her friend. "My sister sent them from the mainland." Vanessa blinked away her guilt at lying and shoved the card back into its envelope. "Wasn't that sweet of her?"

Deflated, Lucy nodded. "Yeah, that's some nice generous sister you have."

Vanessa avoided making eye contact with Lucy. The woman was too astute. "Thanks for bringing them to me."

"I was on my way to your office anyway. So what do you say? Want to go to the Torch tomorrow night for a drink? We'll celebrate your two-week anniversary working at Tempest Maui. My treat."

Vanessa didn't have to think about it. She'd need a night out right after the afternoon wedding fiasco she hoped to create tomorrow. A case of jitters quaked her stomach, but she forged on, noting that besides needing a night out, she could also use a friend. "Sure, I'd love to."

Lucy headed for the door. "I'll pick you up at eight Saturday night. Oh, and don't worry, I won't tell anyone you got flowers from the boss."

Vanessa's jaw dropped open. "How did you—"

"I saw him in the flower shop this morning, handpicking the orchids he wanted in the arrangement."

Contrite, Vanessa slumped her shoulders. "I'm sorry I lied. I didn't want you to get the wrong idea."

"Wrong idea? Are you nuts? Do you know how many women would trade places with you right now?" Lucy winked with a big smile. "You lucky girl."

After she walked out, Vanessa fingered a golden hibiscus, shaking her head. "If Lucy only knew the truth," she whispered to the bird of paradise jutting up from the bouquet. "She wouldn't think I'm lucky. She'd think I'm…insane for going up against the boss."

* * *

"You're drinking white wine?" Lucy said, over the blasting music of the three-piece band at Joe's Tiki Torch. The crowded beachside bar lent itself to loud chatter and laughter amid the patrons. "You should be more adventurous, Vanny. Try an Amaretto Sour or a Mojito or the cliché Blue Hawaiian."

She *had* been adventurous that afternoon when she sabotaged Brock Tyler's reputation. She'd witnessed the chaos during the wedding and had done her part to rectify the problems making sure it had been too little, too late. She'd accomplished what she'd aimed for and thought she'd feel some sense of wicked satisfaction today. Instead, her nerves went raw and the white wine wasn't doing a thing to calm her queasiness. "Maybe you're right. I'll have a strawberry margarita," she said to the bartender.

Lucy's laughter filled the tiny space they occupied at the bamboo bar. "Oh, that's better. You're getting wild and crazy now."

Lucy's playful sarcasm made her smile. Vanessa wasn't a good companion tonight. She had a good deal on her mind. She'd spoken with her sister today, maybe as a means of justification for what she'd done during the wedding. Melody had answered the phone cheerfully, which brightened Vanessa's mood a bit, though she knew her sister was covering up her heartache. Melody was still devastated and Vanessa loved her all the more for trying to pretend she wasn't, for her sake.

Miles separated them now and Melody didn't know that Vanessa had taken a job working at Tempest Maui. She'd deliberately not divulged that information, offering up a different scenario to her sister. As far as Melody knew, Vanessa had taken a temporary transfer to Hawaii and was still working for her previous employer.

"What's the matter, aren't you having a good time? You refuse to dance and you're moping around like you've lost your best friend."

Vanessa stared into Lucy's dark brown concerned eyes. In just a few weeks, they'd become close and Vanessa wished she didn't have to deceive her along with everyone else she'd met since coming to work for Brock Tyler. But to confide in anyone right now could spell disaster.

"I'm just a little tired. It's been a long week."

Lucy took her hand in hers. "That's why we're here, Vanny. You need to unwind. You know, let your hair down. Why don't you dance?"

"Yes, why don't you?"

Vanessa whirled around and found Akamu standing behind her. The hotel manager had a big smile on his face and she couldn't refuse those beckoning eyes.

"Okay," she said, taking his hand. "Mahalo."

His friend Tony asked Lucy to dance and together the four of them took the dance floor. If Akamu knew anything about what happened at the wedding, he wasn't letting on, so Vanessa didn't bring up the subject.

She wound up having a nice time with Akamu, his friend Tony and Lucy. The foursome had Bono, running and a love of healthy foods in common. When Lucy parked her car outside of her condo, Vanessa was in a much better frame of mind than when the evening had begun.

"Thanks, Lucy. I really had fun tonight. Just what I needed."

"Yeah, it took you a while, but you finally lightened up."

"I even tried a Mojito. It was pretty good, though the mint surprised me."

"Who could go wrong with rum, mint and sugar?"

They exited the car and Lucy met her by the passenger door. "I didn't want to bring it up earlier, but I heard what happened at the wedding today."

"Oh, yeah. How did you hear about it?"

"Word travels fast around here. Akamu knew all about it, but his policy is to keep work separate from playtime. I couldn't get much out of him."

"Gosh, he didn't say anything to me." Vanessa sighed. "The wedding wasn't a major disaster or anything." Well, she surmised, it could have been much worse. "But can we talk about it another time? I don't want to spoil my good mood."

Lucy smiled wide and hugged her. "Sure. As long as you're okay."

"I will be. I was feeling a bit homesick today…I miss my sister. Going out was just what I needed tonight."

"You'll get used to being on the island," Lucy said with compassion.

"Thank you. I'll see you on Monday."

"Right, Monday it begins all over again." Lucy rolled her eyes, making Vanessa laugh as they parted.

She strolled leisurely into the garden area of the development with a lingering smile on her face, a bright gleam of moonlight reflecting off the almond-shaped pool. She'd almost made it to her condo, when a man stepped out of the shadows.

"Oh," she gasped in fear, seeing anger on his face. He must know the truth. *She'd been caught.* "Brock, what are you doing here? You scared me half to death."

# Three

Brock paced in front of her, ignoring the fact that she'd nearly jumped out of her skin when he'd come out of the shadows. "I was called back from a meeting I had in Kapalua. Apparently, we had quite a few complaints about the wedding today. Are you aware of what happened?" A frown settled on Brock's face.

Vanessa had dreaded this conversation, but she'd mentally prepared herself. In her preparations, though, she never dreamed he'd come to her home to reprimand her. She walked past him to her door and unlocked it. "Come in. We don't have to discuss this outside in the dark."

Vanessa entered, allowing Brock to follow her

inside and moved about the room, turning lights on and tossing her purse on the sofa.

Brock stood stock-still, a tick working his jaw. "I called your cell phone half a dozen times tonight."

"I turned it off after work." She cast him a quick smile. "I wouldn't have heard it where I went tonight anyway."

"Joe's Tiki Torch?"

"How did you know that?"

"It's the local hangout." He rubbed the back of his neck and added, "I spoke with Akamu tonight."

From his stance, it didn't appear that Brock would leave anytime soon, so she resigned herself to this confrontation. "Have a seat." She turned toward the kitchen. "I'll make a pot of coffee."

"Not for me," he said, following her. "Do you have something to drink?"

"Wine, beer and I think there's a bottle of rum in the cabinet."

"Rum," he said. "And Coke?"

"That, I have." Vanessa opened the kitchen cupboard and reached for the bottle sensing Brock standing right behind her. "Coke's in the fridge."

He moved away to open her refrigerator while she brought down a glass tumbler and poured him a few fingers of rum. He moved in close and filled the rest of the glass with the soda. Their shoulders brushed and his close proximity curled her toes. The male earthy scent of sandalwood filled the air and tension crackled with *his* anger and *her* awareness of him. "None for you?"

She shook her head. "No, I'd better not. I've had enough tonight. Would you like some des—"

"Sit down, Vanessa." He pointed to her kitchen chair and she thought for sure her goose was cooked.

She sat and he did, too, facing her across the small glass table. "What the hell happened today?"

Maybe she should have poured herself a drink after all. Her throat dry, she steadied her nerves. "Well, a lot of things *happened.* Although there were some minor inconveniences, the wedding went off without a hitch."

"Minor inconveniences? You call construction noises during the ceremony a minor inconvenience? That construction wasn't supposed to start until next month."

"I know, but their invoice had a typo on it. They got the date wrong. They started work on the west wing, by mistake."

"I'm told the buzz saw alone drowned out the wedding march music, just as the bride walked down the aisle. She got rattled and started crying. It took thirty minutes to finally find the entire crew and convince them to stop working."

"You're telling me?" Vanessa said, quite adamantly. "I was the one tracking down the supervisor and ordering the stoppage. It was an unfortunate error and we did our best to accommodate the bride and groom after that. Let me tell you that supervisor was not happy.

He had to pay those men regardless, even after I sent them all packing. I'm truly sorry that the bride was distraught, Brock. We did the best we could, under the circumstances."

Brock scratched his jaw and sighed deeply. "I suppose. But that wasn't all. The Garden Pavilion restrooms were stopped up. All the guests were inconvenienced by having to use the restrooms at the far end of the hotel lobby."

"Plumbing problems are the worst." Vanessa nodded her agreement. "We had a team working on it and finally got it all fixed before the reception ended."

"A little late, wouldn't you say?"

Vanessa bit down on her lip. She had to watch her step with Brock. He wasn't a fool. Far from it. "I can assure you, I was on top of all the problems from the moment they occurred."

"It's your job to see that they don't occur." Brock sipped his drink, eyeing her over the glass rim.

"Were there any more complaints?" she asked.

"Weren't those enough? The wedding ceremony nearly ruined and plumbing problems during the entire affair makes for a bad first impression."

"For me? Surely, I couldn't have controlled those things, not even if I were a mind reader." She defended quite convincingly, she thought.

Brock looked deep into her eyes. "No, I didn't say that. It makes for a bad impression for the hotel. Word of mouth is worth a bundle on the island. I only hope comping their honeymoon stay will make it up to them."

"That's a nice gesture."

"Costly." He shrugged. "It's expected when things go wrong."

"I'm sorry there were problems. But I don't think the hotel will suffer too much. Tempest has a good reputation." That much was true and Vanessa aimed to make sure Brock's hotel would become the black sheep of the Tempest flock.

"I'd like to keep it that way." He rose and when she thought he was ready to leave, he walked over to the kitchen counter and poured another drink, mixing rum with Coke again. Then he leaned against the corner of the counter and folded his arms, his gaze focusing directly on her. "Did you enjoy your night out?"

Vanessa rose from her seat, irritated by her vulnerability. She mustered her courage, commending herself on her bravado thus far. Brock made her nervous, especially when his eyes followed her every movement. "Yes, it was a nice evening."

"Did you dance?"

She nodded and leaned opposite him against the counter. "A little. It was nice to unwind."

Brock's gaze flowed over her leisurely, taking in her silvery dress and high-heeled sandals. "I'd like to see that, too. You…unwinding."

Her throat went as dry as tropical wind.

"Truth is, I was in a devil of a mood when I got here, Vanessa."

"Ready to take my head off?" she asked, squeamishly.

"Ready to take something off," he said quietly.

Goose bumps prickled her skin and she remained silent. Even as he set his glass down on the counter. Even as he walked toward her. Even as he stood toe-to-toe with her, her back to the granite countertop, she remained silent.

"My mood is improving," he said, touching a curling strand of her hair and looking down at her mouth.

Her heart raced. She didn't know what to do. She'd been successful in sabotaging him today and now, as he bent his head, oh Lord, she wanted to feel his lips claim hers again. A bizarre, uncanny and…*thrilling* sensation swept clear through her.

"What are—"

His mouth bore down, tasting from her lips again, obliterating her question. He clamped his hands on her hips and pulled her closer, drugging her with his kiss and demanding a response. She couldn't deny his demand, and when he moved closer yet, she wrapped her arms around his neck. "This is crazy," she whispered, the words slipping out.

"Why?" he asked, tugging on her lower lip gently, his sexy sandalwood scent surrounding her senses.

*Because I'm doing my best to ruin you.*

He nipped at her lip again and she sucked oxygen into her lungs, her body reacting to him on every level. The kitchen grew hotter and hotter and when he pressed her mouth open and drove his tongue inside, that heat quickly escalated to sizzling. "I'm not your boss now," he murmured between sweeping kisses.

"What are you then?" she whispered as his tongue explored and tantalized.

"A man completely drawn to you."

"You don't know me, Brock," she said, the conversation taking place between hot, hungry, wet kisses.

"I'm a good judge of character, honey," he said, moving from her mouth to nibble on her throat. "And I know what I want." His hot breath warmed her and she arched her neck, allowing him complete access. Goodness. Pressed against him, she felt the full measure of what he wanted. His erection stymied her next thoughts. Brock's charm, elegance and raw sexuality enveloped her. She couldn't fight back. His weapons were too powerful.

He moistened her shoulder with his tongue, planting little biting kisses there, his hands on either side of her shoulders now, slipping the straps of her dress down, releasing the material.

Her slinky dress betrayed her and fell down around her breasts. Brock's intake of oxygen thrilled her as his gaze swooped down. "Perfect," he offered, admiring her with open lust.

He reached up and circled her breast, outlining it

gently, his thumb flicking the erect tip, causing rapid, potent and instant desire to flare below her waist.

"Brock," she pleaded, and spoke her thoughts aloud. "We can't do this."

"We're doing it," he said softly, "don't fight it."

He cupped one breast and bent his head, his tongue moist on her nipple.

She moaned with pleasure and dug her fingers into his hair. He continued his lusty assault and Vanessa threw caution to the wind, leaning back and relishing each heated caress with total abandon.

Then the phone rang.

Vanessa blinked her eyes. She didn't get too many calls here. What if it was Melody? The answering machine would give Vanessa away. Melody's voice was earthy, with a little Louisiana accent that couldn't be missed. If she said her name into the answering machine…

Vanessa wasn't ready to give up her quest yet. She didn't want to be discovered by Brock.

The phone rang a second time. She pushed at Brock's chest. "I have to get that."

He looked into her eyes. "Let it ring. Your machine will get it."

Two rings to go and all would be lost.

"No, I'm sorry," she said, sliding along the counter and out of his grasp. "I'm expecting an important call."

She dashed into her bedroom and picked up the

bedside phone, looking at a framed photo of Melody and her, arms wrapped around each other, back in Louisiana. She grabbed the frame and tossed it into her dresser drawer, getting rid of the evidence.

Slamming the drawer closed, she answered out of breath, "Hello."

"Hi! Have you recovered from our little excursion tonight?"

"Oh…hi, Lucy," she stammered, surprised it was her friend who'd called.

"I can't find my wallet. Have you seen it by any chance?"

"Uh, no. I haven't. Maybe you left it at the Torch."

"That's my next call. But I had it when I paid the bill. I can't remember what I did with it after that. Just thought maybe it dropped out of my car when I let you off at your place tonight."

"Gosh, I'm sorry," she said, finally focusing on her friend's dilemma. "I'll look around the complex and call you right back."

"Thanks, you're a doll."

Vanessa hung up the phone and straightened her dress, setting the spaghetti straps back in place. She imagined she looked pretty disheveled, but didn't dare glance in the dresser mirror. She didn't want to see the sex-starved expression on her face.

That's what she attributed her attraction to Brock as—her lack of sex. She hadn't been in a relationship for over a year.

"Was that your important call?" Brock startled her, leaning against the doorjam, his gaze intent.

"Uh, no. But it was something important. Lucy lost her wallet. I have to try to find it outside where she dropped me off."

He eyed her for a minute. Glanced at her bed with a lingering look. Then nodded. "I'll help."

"Oh, you don't have to do that. I'm sure I can—"

"Vanessa, I said I'll help."

His tone held no irritation, thankfully. This evening was confusing enough for her. "Okay. Thank you."

When she brushed past him, he took her hand and drew her up against his body. "We're not through yet." He kissed her quickly and released her. "Not by a long shot. Just thought I'd give you fair warning."

Vanessa considered herself duly warned and walked out of her condo with Brock, realizing how close she'd come to being exposed. She'd been lucky this time.

She couldn't afford any more close calls.

But what worried her more was the close call she'd had in Brock's arms.

They'd come very close to making love.

And Vanessa hadn't the willpower to stop him.

"Just turn those car keys over to me now, Brock, and save yourself the grief." Trent's amused laughter came through loud and clear over the cell phone.

Brock winced, and leaned back in his desk chair, mentally shaking off his brother's gibe, but he couldn't banish the image of Trent's gloating face popping into his mind. "Not on your life, bro. In fact, I don't have a clue what you're talking about."

Trent laughed again, grating on Brock's nerves. "Right. Hell, the Everett wedding even made our Arizona papers. I've got the exact words here, 'Jackhammers drowned out the wedding march and brought tears to the hopeful bride's face, the Everett marriage getting off to a dismal start at Tempest Maui's plush, but chaotic, Garden Pavilion.'"

Brock ran his hand down his jaw and heaved a sigh. "Must have been a slow news day at Crimson Canyon. What, you don't have enough going on with your fiancée, you have to call and harass me?"

"Julia says hello, by the way," Trent said good-naturedly. "She told me not to torment you, so I'm letting you off the hook. Just try to do better. You're making this too easy for me."

"Funny, Trent." Brock liked a good challenge, and winning ownership of his late father's classic Thunderbird was part of the deal. He'd bet Trent his newly renovated hotel would make more money in the first year of operation than Trent's western-themed Tempest West. Now, the competition was in full swing. And his pride and reputation were on the line. "Give Julia a kiss for me."

"That, I'll be darn happy to do."

After he hung up the phone, Brock tried concentrating on work, but he couldn't get his mind off Trent's annoying phone call. Brock had worked extremely hard on renovating the hotel, trying to take a failing enterprise and make it a success. He'd hired a new staff and had faith in their abilities. He knew his management team was top-notch. He couldn't afford any more mistakes to be made.

Vanessa entered his mind and he shook his head.

She was competent, hard-working and gorgeous.

She'd been on his mind a lot lately, breaking into his thoughts at the oddest moments. He'd seen her around the offices but they hadn't spoken in two days, since that night when he'd nearly undressed her and taken her to bed. Intoxicating thoughts of what would have happened had they not been interrupted came to mind frequently. He couldn't remember a time he'd enjoyed being with a woman more.

He leaned forward at his desk and buzzed his secretary. "Rosalind, I need a meeting with Vanessa Dupree. Have her come up at noon."

"Okay, Mr. Tyler."

Brock glanced at his watch. Then concentrated on the contracts on his desk, filling the time with work until he'd confront Vanessa.

Hoping to finish what they'd started the other night.

"You wanted to see me?" Vanessa said, entering Brock's office, her mind reeling. She hadn't spoken with him since the night of the wedding fiasco. The night she'd managed to ward off his advances. Considering that entire day had been a lose-lose situation for him, she'd steered clear of him in every way possible. But she couldn't ignore a meeting at the boss's request.

He stood by the window, with his back to her, gazing out at the deep aqua-colored waters of the Pacific, the office view the best in the hotel. His hands thrust in the pockets of his casual tan trousers, he turned around slowly and they made eye contact.

Jarred by the jolting impact of coming face-to-face with him again, Vanessa stood rooted to the spot. She fought her crazy, unwarranted attraction to him, and ignored the dark intensity of his eyes and the ease of his stance.

"Close the door, Vanessa."

She turned and resisted the urge to flee, shutting the door as asked.

"Did you want to talk about the fashion show gala?" She stepped farther into his office.

"Do you have it under control?"

She nodded. "Yes, I'm confident it'll go off as planned." As *she'd* planned, she didn't add. She had more work to do to ensure failure for that event as well.

"Then, no. I have every confidence that you'll make the hotel look good."

"Thank you."

He came forward and sat on the edge of his desk, his long legs crossed at the ankle and smiled. "You're welcome."

They spoke civilly as if their last encounter hadn't been hot and heavy and sexually charged. As if Brock hadn't worked magic on her mouth and hadn't stripped down her clothes and her defenses, nearly making her succumb to his desire.

Thank heaven Lucy had good timing. That phone call had saved her. Vanessa hadn't counted on Brock's attraction to her or the unnerving, completely unwelcome attraction she had for him.

She steeled her resolve. Brock was, in fact, the enemy and she wasn't nearly through with him yet. This was one time the tycoon wouldn't get what he wanted. But with his gaze steady on hers, she couldn't think straight much less breathe.

"Did you need me for something else then?" she asked, fully aware of his close proximity, the scent of sandalwood an unsettling reminder of the other night.

His gaze flicked over her, taking in her aqua-blue knit tank top and white pants and she wondered if her clothes were *too* casual now. The turquoise gemstone necklace draped on her chest seemed to catch his attention, but after a "duh" moment, she realized it wasn't the stone that he admired.

"Yes, I need you. Can you clear your calendar this Saturday night?"

She gulped and blurted, "Why? Are you asking me out on a date?"

One side of his mouth quirked up. "No."

Confused and embarrassed, she blinked, feeling

heat burn its way up her throat. “Oh,” she said, shaking her head, befuddled. “What do you need then?”

“I’ve been invited to the Hawaiian Hotel Association’s annual dinner. There’ll be good opportunity for networking and as my event planner, I think you should join me. Are you free that evening?”

“No. Yes. I mean I’d planned on working on the Fashion Show Gala all day and into the night.”

Brock assessed her with discerning eyes. “You’ll get it done in enough time. The dinner’s at seven and I’ll make sure to have you tucked into bed early.”

Vanessa’s blood ran cold. She needed that time to work on unraveling Sunday’s fashion show. But she really couldn’t refuse Brock’s invitation. She was being squeezed tight between the proverbial rock and the hard place and needed to come up for air. Her mind worked quickly and finally she figured out a Plan B for her sabotage.

Brock stared at her. “Vanessa?”

She hadn’t missed the “I’ll make sure to have you tucked into bed early” comment either. Lurid images popped into her reckless mind.

“It’s just that the other night, things got a little out of control at my place.”

“No, they didn’t.” He lifted up from his perch on the desk to stand straight, arms folded, and surveyed her. “If you were being honest with yourself, you’d say they were right on track.”

She snapped her head up and thought of Melody

and all he'd put her through. She wouldn't qualify his statement with an answer. "This is only a business dinner, right?"

He nodded, making no apologies for the other night. "Absolutely. And it's important."

"Okay, I'll clear my calendar."

"Thank you. And, Vanessa, this is one time it's *not* casual attire."

She granted him a reluctant smile. "I'll make sure to leave my jogging suit at home." Then she walked out the door.

# Four

Brock exited his sterling silver Mercedes and walked up the steps to Vanessa's condo, reflecting on his choice to drive tonight rather than use his limousine. He wanted to be completely alone with Vanessa before and after the dinner with no interruptions. He wanted her all to himself.

She was resistant to his charms and posed a challenge that excited him. Not that other women hadn't turned him down, but with due modesty, those women had been few and far between. Women flocked to Brock and he'd known it was his charm, decent good looks and his pocketbook that impressed them. It was different with Vanessa Dupree. None of that seemed to matter to her.

In fact, more often than not, she seemed completely unimpressed with him. He found himself less irritated at that and more amused and mystified.

Brock straightened his ink-black Armani jacket, tightened the knot of his tie and knocked on her door.

She made him wait. He knocked again and she called out, "Just a sec."

It was worth the wait. Vanessa opened the door and the sight of her made his groin twitch. He lifted his brows and assessed her for a few moments. Her rich platinum hair was full, away from her lovely face and touched her shoulders in soft barrel-like curls. She wore a red strapless dress that hugged her torso and fell along the curves of her hips, draping down her legs with one side riding midthigh in a slit that would catch every male eye in the room.

And Brock would be the man bringing her home.

"You look beautiful," he said.

"It's not too much?" she asked with modesty. "I wasn't sure how 'not casual' you meant."

He glanced at her tempting cherry-red glossy lips and wished there was time to suck the gloss off and kiss her senseless. "You're a perceptive woman, Vanessa. You got it just right. Actually, perfect."

"Hardly that, but thanks for the compliment. You look very nice," she said, her gaze flowing over him for a moment. "Would you like to come in?"

He winced. "With the way you look tonight, it'd be

better if we left right now or I doubt we'd get out of your place until midnight."

She chuckled, thinking he was teasing, no doubt, until she gazed deep into his eyes and saw the truth. Then she nodded, a somber look crossing her features. "I'll get my purse."

She looked just as enticing from the backside and when she grabbed her beaded red purse and turned toward the door, it was all Brock could do from sweeping her off her feet and carrying her into the bedroom.

"Ready?" she asked when she reached him.

"Yeah." He was ready. For her. But he'd have to resign himself to a business dinner for now.

They walked through the flowered gardens and passed the pool in silence, Brock leading her with a hand to the small of her back. His fingers itched to touch more of her and he was glad he'd made the decision to drive his car, rather than be chauffeured. He needed to do something with his hands.

"Did Lucy ever find her wallet?" he asked, making idle conversation. Vanessa's soft fragrant perfume was like an erotic elixir. He needed the distraction of a conversation.

"Yes, she'd left it at the Torch. Lucky for her. I once lost my wallet and it was weeks before I got all my records and credit cards straightened out. I had to cancel everything and start from scratch. What a pain. It's a good thing my sister…uh…never mind. I'm boring you."

Brock chuckled. "No, you're not. I didn't know you had a sister. Younger? Older?"

"Um, younger."

"With pretty platinum hair just like yours?"

"No, my sister looks nothing like me." Brock couldn't miss the way her body stiffened at the mention of her sister.

"Are you close to her?" he asked, drawing her out. He found himself enthralled with all aspects of Vanessa's life. Maybe because she offered so little about herself and that intrigued him.

"Not really. No. She and I have nothing in common." Vanessa clutched her tiny purse tight and she seemed very uncomfortable with the subject. "It's sort of a sore subject right now. We, uh, we don't really get along."

"Okay, fair enough." Brock opened the door for her and watched her glide into her seat, the slit in her dress showing a fair amount of gorgeous leg. "No more questions about your sister."

He shut her door and inhaled deeply, tamping down his lust. He reminded himself once again that this was a business dinner and not a date, though the lower half of him was having trouble remembering that.

He got into the car and started the engine, looking over at Vanessa struggling to put her seatbelt on. "Let me. It can be tricky."

He reached across her body, his arm brushing up against her soft bare shoulder, pulled the belt taut and clamped it into the lock.

"Thank you," she breathed out.

He was close enough to hear the quiet intake of her breath. Satisfied that he affected her to some degree, he returned to his position and drove away with a smug smile tipping the corners of his mouth. "My pleasure, Vanessa."

The dinner couldn't be over soon enough. Brock had plans for Vanessa that included pleasure for both of them.

Clearly, Brock Tyler was the most handsome man at the dinner, if Vanessa were to make a judgment call. Female heads turned when he walked into a room and she noted more than a few envious stares from the women she passed as they made their way to the luxurious circular bar in the corner of the anteroom.

Hundreds of elegantly dressed guests milled about, their laughter and chatter rising above the soft melodic music playing. Crystal chandeliers lit the room and island flowers were displayed in stunning exotic arrangements. The pleasing subtle scent of plumeria graced the air and for the first time all day, Vanessa relaxed.

She sipped a sour apple martini as Brock introduced her to the owners, regional managers and corporate heads of major hotels on the islands. Brock included her in all his conversations, asking her opinion and making her feel on the same level with the moguls who ran the hotel industry. They spent the next forty-five minutes in the upscale bar, but Vanessa could tell Brock was getting impatient.

They slipped away from a small group, Brock's hand warm to her back as he led her to an outer hallway. "Enough networking for a while," he said, sipping his gin and tonic while focusing his attention on her.

He'd gotten her a second sour apple martini, which she carefully nursed. She couldn't afford to lose her inhibitions or her nerve. The big fashion show gala would need her undivided attention tomorrow.

"You don't like schmoozing? You do it so well." And that was the truth. Brock knew how to charm people and make them laugh with his wit and intelligence.

"So I've been told," he said with a chuckle. "But I thought you'd had enough. These dinners can be boring, but necessary."

"Me? Do I look bored?" She didn't want to give off a bad impression and arouse suspicion.

"No, you look…gorgeous."

"I wasn't—"

"I know, you weren't fishing for compliments." He leaned in and placed a delicious kiss on her mouth. When he backed away, his beautiful dark eyes held undeniable promise. "I've wanted to do that all night."

Her stomach went queasy. If Brock bottled his sex appeal, he wouldn't have to run a major hotel chain. He'd make millions in another way entirely.

"You do that so well, too," she muttered.

"Thank you. Coming from you, it's a big compliment."

She tilted her head to the side. "Why do you say that?"

Brock ran his finger along her cheek, tracing the line of her jaw ever so gently, causing prickly goose bumps to rise up on her arms.

"Because you're resisting me."

"And women don't ever resist you?" she asked, keeping her tone light and flirtatious. She couldn't reveal what she really thought about him.

Amused, he grinned and that smile stole her breath. "Now that's a question I'm smart enough not to answer."

"You're my boss," she said quietly.

"You keep saying that, Vanessa. We're both adults and I'm interested in you…more than I've been in a woman in the past decade."

Her queasy stomach clenched. Her heart raced. If it was a line, he'd delivered it convincingly. Vanessa quelled the jarring jolt his admission had to her system. She told herself not to be immensely flattered. She told herself not to believe him. He'd left Melody hurt and alone to pursue another woman.

Yet, there was something in his expression that begged to differ with her innermost thoughts.

She remained silent so long that Brock glanced at his watch. "It's time for dinner."

She smiled weakly and when he took her arm, she walked beside him into the main dining room.

Two hours later, Vanessa found herself in Brock's capable arms on the dance floor. The ballroom's lights dimmed, they danced to a smooth soft ballad that set a mood for romance.

She'd endured dinner and an awards presentation where honors were given out to hotels of excellence in service and guest relations. She'd seen Brock's eyes alight with determination watching the presenters give high honors to his competitors. He wanted his hotel not only to succeed, but to be ranked highest on the islands.

Brock Tyler always had to have the best.

It was a noble ambition for a man who loved his profession. She couldn't fault him there, Brock was diligent, hard-working and fully in command. His employees respected him. They thought him fair and forthright. Being an insider now, she'd heard plenty around the hotel about Brock. Unfortunately, she'd had to listen to female employees spout off about how "hot" Brock was and how they'd love to be one of his overnight guests on his yacht. They'd seen that yacht take off plenty of nights and all had surmised without a doubt that he hadn't been alone.

Vanessa had always kept quiet when the conversation turned to Brock, but she'd taken it all in and was reminded that Brock wasn't to be trusted no matter how charming he could be.

"You're quiet tonight," he said, holding her at a respectable distance.

"Just being a good listener."

Brock brought her slightly closer. "That's a good quality in a woman," he said quite seriously.

She lifted her head up to meet his eyes and saw a mischievous grin surface on his face. She shook her head. "There's a few feminist organizations who'd tar and feather you for saying that."

"Hmmm, I think I've met some of those women already. They don't like me."

"I don't doubt it," she said, feeling justified.

Brock brought her closer yet and whispered in her ear. "I only care about one woman liking me."

A shocking thrill coursed through her body. As much as she wanted to be immune to him, there was something so incredibly charismatic about him. "I…like you, Brock."

He nodded, satisfied. When the music ended, he guided her to the table and they took their seats. Coffee was served and Vanessa was glad that the evening was coming to an end.

Someone tapped Brock on the shoulder and a sultry voice whispered behind him. "Have you been hiding from me all night?"

Vanessa turned her head to find a stunning dark-haired woman with bright green lust-filled eyes, devouring Brock. He rose from his seat to greet her. "Hello, Larissa."

"Hello? Is that all you can say?"

She lifted up and kissed Brock gently on the lips. "There, that's better."

Something powerful tightened in Vanessa's stomach. She turned away for a second, to smile at the other eight people seated at the table. Had she imagined it, or did they all look at her with sympathetic eyes?

"Why haven't you called?" Vanessa heard the woman question him as if no one existed at the table but Brock.

Brock hesitated to answer for a second. "Vanessa," he said, and she closed her eyes briefly before turning around to glance at him. "Will you excuse me? I'll be right back."

"Of course. Take your time."

Brock nodded and excused himself to the others seated at their table. Vanessa watched him walk away with Larissa on his arm.

Fiona Davis, the older woman seated next to her, laid a gentle hand on her arm. "She's the Association president's daughter. I wouldn't worry too much. She's engaged, though she is a bit of a flirt."

"Oh, I'm not worried," Vanessa blurted. "I mean to say, this isn't what it looks like. Mr. Tyler is my employer. We're here on business."

Fiona sent her a motherly smile and said quietly, "Maybe you are, but he hasn't taken his eyes off you all evening. He's eligible, handsome as the devil and rich.

I wouldn't dismiss his interest in you so easily." Fiona sighed longingly. "Dare I say the old cliché, he's a catch?"

Vanessa stared into Fiona's soft brown eyes. "What if I'm not fishing?"

She smiled knowingly. "Ah, you don't want to get involved. Someone hurt you?"

"Yes," Vanessa admitted. She'd been hurt in the past. She'd been dumped for another woman when she was younger more than once. She'd lost her high school sweetheart to a girl with an IQ of a snail. Later on, she figured they deserved what they'd gotten since they'd cheated on each other and wound up hating one another. And in college, she'd almost gotten engaged, until she found her would-be fiancé in bed with her roommate. The shock had crippled her for a time and made her wary of men, but she'd gotten over the hurt long ago. This time, it wasn't about her. She was doing this for Melody—standing up for her sister, who'd been devastated by Brock Tyler's hurtful dismissal of her. "I've been hurt before. And it's too soon for another involvement."

She'd transposed Melody's hurt onto herself for Fiona's benefit. It made her feel less like a liar to the kindhearted woman. Lord knows she'd lied to enough people since she'd come to the island.

"I understand. Before I met my late husband, I had a crushing experience."

For fifteen minutes, Vanessa listened to Fiona speak

about her past hurts and how she'd managed to recuperate from them. They were the last ones left at the table and when Fiona also had to leave, Vanessa bid her farewell and got up to use the ladies' room.

She headed past the anteroom and down the hallway, clutching her purse in her hand, her anger at Brock over his abandonment of her in the ballroom building. When she spotted him outside on the plush grounds, standing arm in arm with the black-haired what's-her-name, she came to a halt, pivoted around abruptly and headed for the lobby where she promptly summoned a cab to take her home.

"Let him look for me," she muttered, then thought better of it. She couldn't afford to get fired. She wrote a quick note and handed it to the valet before getting into the cab. "Give this to Mr. Brock Tyler. He's the one with the silver Mercedes."

She had things to do early in the morning. She didn't want to rush him away from the event. She needed her rest.

That's what she'd written on the note and what she'd tell him tomorrow if asked.

Vanessa ignored the pangs of jealousy she felt seeing him with that woman and hated Brock all the more for making her feel that way.

She rested her head on the back of the cab's seat and closed her eyes, going over her plan for the Fashion Institute's Valentine's Day Gala. "Brock Tyler, you'll get yours tomorrow."

* * *

The doorbell rang three times in succession, the incessant chimes rattling her eardrums. "Just a minute," she called out, tossing her arms through her silk robe and tying the sash. She padded to the door and peeked out the peephole.

Oh, God.

Brock.

"Open the door, Vanessa."

Judging from the tone of his voice and the hard look in his eyes, he wasn't a happy man.

Vanessa filled her lungs with oxygen and opened the door.

"What the hell were you thinking?" Brock didn't wait for an invitation. He entered her humble condo then whirled around on her.

"I don't know what you mean," she answered calmly.

"I mean when I take a woman out, I fully expect to be the one to deposit her back home safely. You walked out on me. I don't think any woman has done that before."

The mystified expression on his face stymied her for a second. Then on impulse, she laughed at the absurdity. "I'm sorry." She covered her hand to her mouth, yet she couldn't hide her amusement. "It's not funny, but you should see the look on your face."

A tick worked his jaw. Obviously, he wasn't amused. "Vanessa, answer my question. Why in hell did you leave?"

"Did you get my note?"

"After searching for you for ten minutes."

Vanessa smiled to herself. He'd been dumped, if even for ten minutes, and he hadn't liked how it felt. Payback could be sheer pleasure at times. "I'm sorry if you were inconvenienced," she said sincerely.

He frowned.

"I told you in the note that I didn't want to hold you up. You were busy with whatever her name was, and I needed to get to bed early tonight."

"Damn it. I was talking business with Larissa Montrayne. She's getting married and wanted to ask me some questions. Do you know what it would mean if she decided to have her wedding at Tempest?"

"It'd be huge?"

"Right. It would be huge."

"But shouldn't those questions have been asked of your event planner? I thought that's the whole reason you brought me with you tonight."

"Larissa needs personal attention. She's…temperamental."

"You mean she's spoiled."

A corner of his mouth cocked up. "Maybe."

"And she wanted *your* undivided attention."

"If you hadn't hightailed it out of Dodge so quickly, you might have had a chance to talk with her. I brought her back to the table and you were gone."

"That must have been awkward." Vanessa pictured that scenario, relishing the images drifting into her mind.

"I was concerned."

"For me?"

"Like I said, no one has ever walked out on me like that."

"So you thought maybe someone kidnapped me? Or maybe I fell and hit my head in the ladies' room?"

Brock drew his brows together. "When I got your note, I was furious."

"You'd rather I'd hit my head and was lying unconscious somewhere?"

He stared at her.

"Are you going to fire me?"

"Fire you?" Again his brows furrowed and he shook his head. "Vanessa, I'm just trying to figure you out."

She shrugged and walked toward the front door, a gesture to let him know it was time to leave. "There's nothing much to figure out. I told you the reason I left."

"Couldn't be that you were jealous?"

Vanessa wrapped her arms tight around her middle and shook her head. "Of course not."

Brock made a move toward the door and she thought he'd finally taken the hint. When he gently closed the door and turned to her, she realized she'd been mistaken. "Larissa thought you were. She apologized for monopolizing my time."

"I bet she did," Vanessa mumbled. That woman's eyes sparkled with glee when she'd successfully orchestrated Brock's sole attention.

He shot her a knowing look. "I was hopping mad

when you took off." His tone mellowed and his gaze flowed over her softly.

"And now?" Vanessa feared his answer.

"Now, I'm flattered."

"Brock, don't tell me your ego needs stroking."

"No, not my ego." He sent her a sinful smile, one filled with so much hunger, her knees buckled.

She turned away from him and tried to block out the tempting look on his face and the way his strong voice had taken on a softer edge.

This was crazy. *She* was crazy. She couldn't let him get to her this way. She had been jealous, which was ridiculous. She'd come to Maui for the sole purpose of ruining his reputation. She'd wanted to hit him where it hurt the most.

"I think you should leave." She whirled around to face him only to find him directly in front of her now, his jacket and tie tossed aside. His shirt unbuttoned at the throat. How had he done that so fast?

Her pulse reeling, she swallowed and blinked her eyes away from the bronzed skin peeking out from his shirt.

Brock laid his hands on her waist and drew her closer, his voice a whisper near her ear. "I'm dying to know what's under this robe."

She wanted to say he'd never find out, but his mouth descended on hers and obliterated all thought. His hands slid from her waist to her derriere and he cupped her, pressing gently and bringing her up against his hips. Her thin silky robe did little to protect her from the strength of his body.

She savored the taste of whiskey and desire on his lips, burning her with his hunger. She met his greedy demand and roped her arms around his neck. His kisses urgent and needy, both of them were wrapped up in a moment of ecstasy.

Brock brought her with him as he stepped backward until he met with the wall. Then he pivoted, taking her with him, until she replaced his position. She arched her head back, and he drizzled hot wet kisses from her lips to her chin, her throat and down to the V of her robe.

She felt a tug and her sash released from the tie. Her robe parted, leaving the center of her body uncovered. Brock glanced at her red lace bra and thong panties and a guttural groan escaped the depths of his throat.

"Vanessa," he whispered with warm breath. "You don't disappoint."

He kissed the valley between her breasts then fingered the lace of her bra, teasing her with light butterfly caresses. She ached for him to touch more of her, to bend his head and mouth her breasts until her nipples pebbled hard.

But instead, he reached down lower, his hand skimming her torso and traveling below her navel. He dipped under her panties and cupped her between the thighs.

"Oh," she sighed softly, the tingling shock and pleasure of his touch creating tremors.

He brought his lips to hers again, claiming her with his tongue and driving deep inside, while he stroked her womanhood slowly, exquisitely.

She closed her eyes and allowed him full access. She grew moist instantly and he stroked her harder, with more demand. She surrendered to his caresses and the tremors built. She moved on him now, her body in rhythm to his delicious mouth and his expert hand. She swayed and rocked back and sighed out her pleasure.

"Brock," she pleaded, her pleasure heightened to the limit.

He continued to stroke her most sensitive spot. "Come for me, honey. Now."

His words threw her over the edge. She splintered into a thousand tiny fragments, her release fast and hard. Breathing heavy, her breasts full and her nerves quaking, she moaned with frenzied delight.

The climax left her boneless. With heavy lids, she opened her eyes to find Brock watching her with a hot steamy gleam in his eyes.

He smiled and kissed her lightly on the lips. "You should see the look on *your* face."

He tossed her comment back at her, and she bit her lip, ready to react, until he added, "It'll haunt my dreams tonight."

He picked up his suit jacket and tie and walked out of her condo.

Leaving her satisfied and wanton, and more than slightly confused.

# Five

Timing was everything in this world but this time it didn't work in Brock's favor. He'd left a willing woman in the throes of passion and walked out on her.

To catch a plane to Los Angeles.

If it had been business instead of a family matter, Brock would have postponed the flight without blinking an eye. He'd be in bed with Vanessa Dupree right now, instead of sitting on the Tempest jet, traveling in the dead of night to make an engagement luncheon in Beverly Hills for his mother and her fiancé, Matthew Lowell.

Vanessa posed a challenge and Brock couldn't remember when he'd had a harder time trying to get a lady interested. She'd been on his mind a lot lately. And tonight he'd planned on a romantic evening and afterward, making sweet love to her.

Damn her for pulling that stunt at the dinner and throwing his well-planned evening into a confused, frustrating mess. If she were anyone else, he'd dismiss her as being more trouble than she was worth. Completely high maintenance, but not in a demanding, spoiled rich-bitch way. No, Vanessa had qualities that unnerved him. She was smart, charming, capable and adept at everything she did. Now that he knew her, now that he'd seen the glint of sizzling passion in her eyes, the way her body rocked sensually to his ministrations, the way little moans of ecstasy escaped her lips, Brock had to know more. He had to have her. Possess her. In every way.

Hell, he *liked* her.

More than he had liked a woman in a very long time.

There was something unique and mystifying about Vanessa Dupree. She'd been hot and ready and seeing her face when she'd combusted in his arms pulled at him in a dozen different ways. He'd been in awe. He'd been shaken.

The thought of making love to her quickly then running to catch a plane didn't appeal to him. He wanted time with her. Enough time to explore every inch of her and drive them both into oblivion. So Brock had left her, never to forget the look of lust on her pretty face, the melting softness in her eyes and the feel of her dewy damp skin under his fingertips, just before he'd walked out the door.

"Go to sleep, Brock," he mumbled as he stretched out on the sofa. As the jet's engine purred, he closed his eyes, banishing any more thoughts of Vanessa and hoping that his prediction tonight wouldn't come true—she wouldn't haunt his dreams.

The following morning, Brock exited his hotel room at Tempest Beverly Hills and met his family precisely at noon in a small private elegant dining room.

He came up behind his mother and pulled her into his arms. "Hi, Mom."

Rebecca turned around and smiled. "Brock, you made it."

The warm glow in her eyes and the happiness on her face told Brock all he needed to know—Matthew Lowell was a fine man. He couldn't replace his father, but he'd make his mother happy and that's what mattered the most. "I wouldn't miss it. Flew all night to get here."

Matthew stepped up and shook his hand. "Brock, glad to see you again."

"Same here." Brock assessed Matthew, who was his brother Trent's soon-to-be father-in-law. The older man had a contented gleam in his eyes. "Congratulations, you're getting a great woman." Brock wrapped his arm around his mother's shoulder and squeezed.

"I know," Matthew said. "I'm a lucky man. I have a

new grandson and when I thought life couldn't get any better, I fell in love."

"He's marrying a grandmother," Rebecca added. "Goodness, I can hardly believe it."

His mother couldn't be more pleased that Evan and Laney had a son and that more grandchildren were probably on the way. Trent and Julia wanted a family, too. Once again, Brock was the black sheep in the Tyler family. Heck, even his best friend, Code, was married and going to be a father. Sarah was halfway through her pregnancy.

Brock wasn't the marrying kind and he'd never thought of himself as father material. It was a good thing that his brothers had picked up the slack.

When Laney and Evan walked in, all focus went to the little boy named after their deceased father, John Charles Tyler.

Rebecca got to the baby first, snuggling him in her arms and bestowing countless kisses. Little Johnny was passed around to all the females in the family first, then Trent took a turn at holding him. He looked good with a child in his arms. *Better him than me,* Brock thought.

"Your turn, bro." Trent walked over to Brock.

"No, thanks. I can see Johnny just fine standing right next to you."

Laney walked over to him. "Now, Brock. Johnny needs to bond with all of his uncles." She took Johnny out of Trent's arms with all the instincts of a confident mother and set the baby in his arms. "There. You're a natural."

"She's right," Evan said, staring down at his son with pride. "You look good with a baby in your arms."

Trent slapped him on the back and grinned like a circus clown. "I couldn't agree more."

Brock made the mistake of glancing at his mother. Her eyes softened on him and little Johnny, and her expression filled with hope. He cleared his throat, quietly so as not to startle the baby who seemed to be studying him with curious blue eyes. "I'm not going down that road."

Evan roped his arms around Laney. "It sort of creeps up on you, Brock. Right, Laney?"

"Right," she agreed.

Julia chimed right in. "I can't wait until we have children."

"You arcn't married yet."

"We will be," Trent said. "That's one reason we all gathered here today. To celebrate Mom and Matthew's engagement and to see if you wouldn't mind hosting our wedding?"

Brock handed the baby back to Laney. He needed to focus on this request. "You want to get married in Maui?"

"We do." Four voices chimed in at the same time.

Brock drew his brows together. "All four of you?"

"That's right," his mother said. "Julia and Trent and Matthew and I thought we'd marry in a double ceremony."

"It's fitting," Matthew said with a bob of his head.

"That's if you think you can keep the bathrooms from overflowing and the noise level down on the beach, bro." Trent's amusement met with a warning stare from Rebecca.

"We have discussed it, dear. We think it's the perfect location," she said.

"I thought you'd want to marry at Crimson Canyon," he said to Julia and Trent.

"Mom wants a tropical wedding on the beach. And Julia and I are fine with it," Trent said. Julia gazed adoringly at her fiancé. "We have our whole lives in the canyon to look forward to."

Trent bent to kiss her lips.

Brock nodded. "Okay, we'll have your wedding at Tempest Maui." Brock realized he didn't sound enthusiastic so he put on a big smile. "It'll be my pleasure and an honor."

If it wasn't a disaster.

The pressure was on. Brock would never live it down if something fouled up the double ceremony. Not that he had any reason to believe so. The first wedding at his Hawaiian resort had been flawed, but they'd since ironed out all the problems. The Fashion Institute's gala should go smoothly today and they'd be on the right track again.

"I'll check with Vanessa, my event planner, when I get back and we'll discuss wedding dates that work for everyone."

An image of Vanessa as he left her last night, half-naked, her eyes a soft glaze of blue and her gorgeous body glistening with the afterglow of her powerful climax stuck in his mind. His groin tightened with a need so dire it shocked him. He pictured her here, with all that platinum hair flowing, laughing beside him as she charmed his family.

The mental picture gave him pause.

"Lunch is ready," Evan said, to Brock's relief. He was grateful for the distraction.

Evan ushered them to their places in the dining room. "Let's discuss the weddings as we celebrate Mom and Matthew's engagement."

"But first, a toast," Brock said, picking up a champagne flute and looking at his family members, their numbers increasing with wives and babies. He was the outsider, the man alone, the sole bachelor in the family and Brock didn't mind at all.

He was in his comfort zone.

Brock wouldn't think of Vanessa Dupree as the woman who would settle him down and have his children.

And that was the biggest comfort of all.

Vanessa rubbed sunscreen on her legs and arms, then lowered herself down on a beach towel and let the Hawaiian rays warm her. It wasn't an overly hot day, but she wouldn't complain. It was February, and back on the mainland where she grew up near Baton Rouge, the temps were in the middle sixties. Here on Maui, the sun shone warm and soaked into her skin with a pleasant heat.

Instead of doing laundry at her condo on her afternoon off, she decided to treat herself to some R & R on the sands of Tranquility Bay. It was a celebration of sorts. She'd gotten really lucky, managing to foul up the fashion gala three days ago while Brock was out of town. Everything had gone as she'd anticipated. The lighting, the slideshow in the background, the seating arrangements, had all mysteriously gone awry, making Tempest Maui look like an amateur high school production rather than the five-star resort that it claimed to be.

She closed her eyes, commending herself on a job well done. If she managed to hold on to her employ long enough, she'd ruin Brock Tyler's business.

At least temporarily. Men like Brock didn't fail. He'd come back strong, she was certain. But as long as she tossed stumbling blocks on his path to success, making his road harder to navigate, she'd be satisfied. It might make him stand up and take notice that people weren't put on this earth for his sole pleasure and entertainment.

The way Melody described how he'd courted her, lavishing her with expensive gifts, treating her like royalty, focusing all his attention on her, thus making her fall head over heels for him, had disgusted her. He'd dumped her sister like a hot potato when he'd met another woman who'd intrigued him more. Vanessa's blood boiled, and the reminder cemented her resolve. She wouldn't allow guilty feelings to intervene. Akamu wouldn't take the heat from this last foul-up. Lucy hadn't been involved. Her new friends were in the clear.

It was all on her. She was the Tempest event planner. The buck stopped here.

She'd lucked out that Brock had been gone these past few days. She hadn't seen or spoken with him since he'd left her rather stunned in her condo on Saturday night. She'd melted into a puddle from his kisses and allowed him liberties far beyond what she'd ever expected to allow.

She squeezed her eyes tight, attempting to block out the memory. Brock had shattered her. He'd made her come alive. She'd splintered before his eyes and she'd come up panting and shamelessly wanting more. The only thing stopping her from dire mortification that night had been the hungry, appreciative look on Brock's face.

He hadn't been proving a point. He hadn't resorted to revenge for her walking out on him after the dinner. No, he'd been fully, deeply involved. He had regret in his eyes when he'd left her. He had wanted to stay. Later, she found out why he'd taken that midnight flight. He wouldn't miss his mother's engagement celebration.

Vanessa rolled onto her stomach and picked up her

cell phone. She punched in Melody's auto-dial number. The phone rang and rang. "Where are you, Melly?" she mumbled, right before her answering machine clicked on.

"Hi! You've reached Melody. You know the drill. I'll get to ya when I can." Melody's beaming voice brought a quick smile to Vanessa's face, before she frowned.

"Hi, Mel, where are you? I've been trying to reach you today. Call your big sister as soon as you can."

Vanessa worried about her sister's state of mind. Melody had been distraught and depressed when she'd left for Maui, but Melody assured her she'd manage. She'd encouraged her to go.

An hour later, sunbathed and more relaxed than she'd been in weeks, Vanessa packed up her beach gear. She bent to pick up her striped beach towel. As she turned around she came face-to-face with Brock. "Oh!"

Where had he come from? With his chest bare, wearing tan shorts and running shoes, she noted he was out of breath. He'd been running on the beach.

He watched her fidget with the items she held in her hand, keeping the towel close to her bikini-clad body. Her face flamed and she decided it was a good thing the sun shone bright today. She'd blame her flush on the heat.

"Hello, Vanessa."

"Um, hi." She gazed out at the aqua waters unnerved

by the way he looked at her. A thought struck. "It's my afternoon off. I wasn't—"

He took the towel from her hands and raked his eyes over her black bikini, or rather the parts of her body the bikini didn't cover. "I know."

They stared at each other for a long moment.

Her traitorous heart flipped over itself. She'd expected fear, loathing or something akin to dismay, seeing him again. But what she felt was…thrilling.

She filled her gaze with him. Why did he have this effect on her?

"Sit down for a minute, Vanessa."

She nibbled on her lower lip. This wasn't a request, but a command.

He set the beach blanket out onto the sand and gestured. She sat, then he sat. Both gazed at the waves rippling to the shore in white froth.

"It's good to see you," he said.

It was the last thing she'd expected him to say. "Thank…you."

*Oh, Lord, Vanessa. Get a grip.*

His shoulder brushed hers. A golden sheen coated his muscled chest. Vanessa was fully aware of him, the faint scent of sandalwood and man oozing from his body.

"I've been gone for three days and frankly, I wasn't happy with how we left things the other night."

"How was that?" she blurted. She wasn't sure what he was getting at and *frankly,* she didn't want this conversation. The irony astounded her. With miles of clear blue seas and pristine sand surrounding her, she felt trapped and couldn't find a way out of this exchange.

"Unfinished."

Vanessa blinked and her nerves jangled. "Maybe," she began, nibbling once again on her lower lip, "it was a good thing that you left when you did."

"I had to go. I didn't want to, Vanessa. I had a midnight flight to catch to the mainland. I don't think you wanted me to go either. I'm usually not a love 'em and leave 'em kind of man."

Liar. Melody's tearful face flashed in her mind.

"Okay." She had to play along. She wasn't finished with Brock yet.

"As long as we're clear about that."

"All clear." She feigned a big smile.

"Now, maybe you can tell me what happened at the fashion gala. I didn't get a glowing report. Quite the contrary, actually."

Vanessa spent the next ten minutes bluffing her way through an explanation. Brock listened intently, nodded his head and asked a few key questions. She'd expected these questions and had rehearsed the answers.

Brock glanced at her lips on several occasions. He lowered his gaze many times, too, his gorgeous dark eyes roaming over her skin.

When she was through explaining her way out of the gala catastrophe, Brock leaned back on his elbows and took a deep breath. "Spend the night with me, Vanessa."

Just like that, he'd voiced his innermost desires and expected her to comply. For a brief moment, the temptation to spend the night in Brock's arms carried in her thoughts. "When?"

"Tonight." She felt the heat of his penetrating gaze on her back.

"I can't. I have plans with...Lucy."

Brock sat up again and gazed into her eyes as if searching her for the truth. "Okay."

She sent him a regretful smile.

Brock's expression changed and he became thoughtful. "I need to take a more active role in the hotel. I've been absent each time we had an important event. Next time, I won't be gone. I expect you to accompany me to the luau on Saturday night. Between the both of us, we'll make sure there are no missteps."

Now, her goose *was* cooked. "That's a good idea."

Brock stood and looked at her. Then he reached down, his hand outstretched. She slid her hand in his and he drew her upright and into his arms smoothly. His hands splayed over her waist. "Just so we're clear," he repeated, before dipping his head and slanting his lips over hers. Their bodies brushed, her breasts covered in the slightest cotton material, pressed his chest.

The kiss nearly buckled her knees. When he broke off the kiss and gazed into her eyes, she nodded and managed, "Very clear."

# Six

Vanessa adjusted her pareo around her body in the most flattering way possible. She tied the black material garnished with printed white gardenias slightly above her breasts into a bow the way Lucy had shown her. The sarong fell to just below her knees in an elegant angle.

"There," she said, looking at her reflection in the mirror. "Not bad for a mainlander."

Once satisfied with the dress, Vanessa swept her hair up in a twist and placed a fresh orchid behind her right ear, pinning it in place. She applied pink lip gloss, slanted a mascara wand over her lashes a few times and slipped her feet into a pair of strapless sandals.

"All set for the luau?" Lucy walked into the room, sipping on a fruit smoothie.

Vanessa turned away from the mirror to face her friend. "How do I look?"

"The pareo was made for you," Lucy said, coming to stand beside her. "You look like an island princess, Waneka."

Vanessa smiled as the phonetic Hawaiian name rolled off Lucy's lips. With Lucy's long raven hair and her dark natural skin tone, she was the true island beauty. "You fit the part better, Luana."

Lucy shrugged. "I bet Mr. Tyler doesn't think so. You're the one he's always watching."

*Because he's suspicious of me,* Vanessa thought wryly. Or maybe her guilty conscience was in overdrive tonight. Because, this evening her friends would be *involved.* Tonight, Akamu would oversee the food preparations and Lucy was in charge of the entertainment.

Brock was getting what he deserved, but her friends might take the heat when things got chaotic during the luau and Vanessa cringed at that thought.

She and Lucy drove separately to the hotel, Lucy giving her a knowing look when she explained that Brock insisted that she accompany him to the event for business reasons.

Once she arrived, she headed for his office and knocked on Brock's door.

"Come in," he said, and she found him at his desk, flipping through a batch of papers.

When he looked up, his eyes took on a warm glow. "Wow." He rose from his seat and walked around his desk. She wanted to exclaim "wow," too, but held her tongue. He looked like the millions she knew he had, casual but classy in tan slacks and a black silk shirt. He'd combed his dark hair back, accentuating strong bone structure and those knockout deep brown eyes.

Vanessa's blood surged in her veins. Her boss was sexy and she wasn't immune. The air sizzled around them, the sweetly fragrant Hawaiian scents adding allure to a room filled with tension.

"You look...*almost* perfect." He stood before her and reached for the orchid in her hair, removing it from her right ear. He placed it behind her left ear and nodded his approval. "Now, it's perfect."

Vanessa touched her hair, questioning him silently.

"Wearing it on the left side means the woman is taken."

"Oh." The explanation stunned her for a moment. His implication was clear.

He smiled and toyed with the bow around her breasts. One manly tug and her dress would be a gossamer puddle around her feet. "Do you know the restraint I'm managing, not to unravel you out of this dress."

Vanessa swallowed. "It's called a pareo."

Brock grinned. "You're learning." Then his eyes darkened to an even deeper brown. "But that's not my point."

For a fleeting moment, she wanted to be unraveled out of her sarong and tossed onto his desk caveman-style, disregarding all sense of reason.

He lowered his voice. "It would be so easy, Vanessa." He tugged on the sash beneath the bow gently. "Would you like that?"

Vanessa blinked and then closed her eyes. Oh, God. She would *love* it.

His lips brushed hers tenderly and she snapped her eyes open. But the kiss was so breathtakingly good she closed her eyes again, wrapped her arms around his neck and simply enjoyed the taste of Brock and his subtle sandalwood scent that made her heart beat like crazy.

His hands caressed her derriere and he deepened the kiss, applying pressure to her lips. Bringing her up close, he rubbed her against his rising manhood and she moaned longingly, the sound escaping before she could stop it.

"Damn, Vanessa," he whispered, breaking off his kiss and the hold he had on her. "Don't make plans for later tonight. We're going to finish this."

He took her hand and led her out of his office, heading outside as the sun set in orange hues over Tranquility Bay.

Ten minutes later disaster struck…right on cue. Brock stood beside her and Akamu on the hotel's private beach lit by tiki torches when all hell broke loose. He glanced at the reservation book. "There's at least one hundred extra people waiting in line, all claiming to have made reservations. Their names are not on our list." He yanked off the orchid lei from his neck and stared at Vanessa.

She heard the buzz of irate conversations from the people waiting in line and her stomach churned. Brock waited for her response.

"I don't get it. We've verified all the names on the guest list. We only signed up two hundred. We're not equipped for this many people. I'll turn them away with our deepest apologies."

That had been her plan. Turn them away disgruntled. Word of mouth would spread like wildfire.

"They're not going to like that. Those people are hungry and cranky, boss." Akamu shook his head and gazed at the line, his eyes wide with horror.

"What's your solution then?" Brock glanced from Akamu to Vanessa. "Well?"

"I'm sorry, I have no idea how this happened." Vanessa's apology met with deaf ears. "Maybe a computer glitch?" She'd managed to sabotage the guest book, deleting names and adding to the list all week long. It hadn't been difficult. "We could invite them back tomorrow night."

Brock's jaw tightened. "No. We're going to accommodate them tonight."

Vanessa's brows shot up in surprise. "How?"

He turned to Akamu. "Get into the kitchen. Have the chefs prepare one hundred more servings of side dishes. Make some calls to local restaurants. Beg and borrow, steal if necessary, fifty pounds of Kalua pig. Vanessa, you get housekeeping out here and have them set up any tables they can get their hands on. We won't turn these guests away. I'll make the rounds and speak with them myself. Let them know they'll be my guests for a complimentary breakfast on the beach tomorrow."

Akamu and Vanessa nodded.

"Go," he ordered and Vanessa saw the look of disdain on his face. She suspected Brock Tyler didn't like apologizing to anyone about anything.

Her insides knotted with tension. She'd never been a witness to Brock's wrath, but he was certainly not happy with her right now.

This may very well be her last night on the job.

Brock settled the mess at the luau and sat down more than an hour later, finally grabbing a bite to eat. Vanessa had been quiet though diligent in getting the extra guests seated and fed. It had taken nearly an entire hour, delaying the meal and the performances, to appease one hundred grumpy guests. Many were still not happy with their seats or the situation.

A strange wary feeling stormed his gut and he looked at Vanessa, seated across from him, eating mochiko chicken. She looked so beautiful and so…aloof. When she glanced at him, he couldn't read those deep sea-blue eyes.

The disaster had been averted somewhat. Brock had seen to it, but the damage had been done. Those additional guests had gotten a raw deal and Brock wasn't happy about that. The fact that his first important hotel events had been faulty, churned in his stomach.

His pride and ego were on the line.

Trent would never let him live it down if he didn't come out the winner.

And Brock hated losing.

Had he let his desire for Vanessa cloud his judgment? She'd come with impeccable references. He knew she was sharp as a whip. So what was up? How had these three hotel events become minidisasters?

They sat at a back table watching the hula performers mesmerize the crowd, and every so often two pairs of male eyes glanced at Vanessa, darting her interested looks when they thought no one was watching. Brock couldn't *blame* the men seated at their table. Vanessa wasn't just another pretty face, she had something unique—a Marilyn Monroe appeal with pouty lips and luminous platinum hair that begged to be touched.

He couldn't *blame* the men for looking her way, but he didn't like it.

Nor did he like the rush of possessiveness he felt about her. Hell, they hadn't slept together yet and he was casting innocent men cold, hard, she's-mine looks.

Had he let his lust for Vanessa mar his good instincts?

As much as he didn't want to believe it he had strong suspicions about Vanessa Dupree's actions of late.

"I think we averted the disaster," she said, licking chicken drippings off her fingers. Brock watched her tongue wrap around her index finger, then shot a narrow-eyed warning at the bald-headed father of four, who found Vanessa's mouth a little too fascinating.

"You think?" Brock shook his head. "I'm not sure."

"Well, at least we provided seats and food for everyone."

"Cost the hotel a bundle. Our competitors soaked us for the pork dishes they provided. Can't host a luau without Kalua pig and they took advantage."

"I'm sorry, Brock."

She did sound sincere. "How sorry?"

She tilted her head and glanced at him directly. "How sorry do you want me to be?"

He may have a reputation as being a playboy, but Brock wasn't the kind of man who exchanged sexual favors for anything other than pleasure. He wanted Vanessa, but not that way. Not that he thought for a second she was offering. She hadn't made his pursuit easy and he'd backed off enough to give her time to decide what she wanted.

Now, trust was an issue. He didn't know why, but he had a bad feeling about this. He rose from his seat. "I've got to go over receipts with Akamu. I'll leave you in charge here."

"Okay. I've got it under control."

Brock stared at her for a moment, then made sure the wandering eyes at the table met with his stony gaze. "I'll be back soon."

*Hell,* he thought. *She's got me acting like a love-struck teenager.*

Yet Brock had to put his suspicions to rest. He spent a minute speaking with Akamu, then headed straight for his office. Once inside, he closed the door and called his friend Code Landon.

"I need a favor, Code. That's if you can tear yourself away from Sarah long enough to help a friend."

"Sarah's busy in the studio working on an album."

"I thought she retired from show business. What's up? You can't keep your wife home these days?"

Code laughed. "Not in this lifetime, buddy. I built her an in-home studio. She's making a record of lullabies for the baby. Pouring her heart and soul into it. I've never heard anything so beautiful."

The change in Code's demeanor since he fell for Sarah Rose was almost tangible. The onetime bitter, confirmed bachelor was now a happily married man with a child on the way. Brock had been his friend since childhood. There wasn't anyone he trusted more, outside of his own brothers. "You hit the jackpot, Code."

"I know. You should try it sometime."

Brock flinched. The woman who entered his mind first and foremost was the one he had undeniable suspicions about. The one he would beseech his best friend to investigate. "Hey, someone has to represent the bachelors of the world."

"Man, you don't know. You just don't know. Now, about that favor, lay it on me. Sarah's gonna want my undivided attention as soon as she's through."

"Vanessa Dupree. I need to know everything there is to know about her. And I need it, yesterday."

"Okay. Give me what you've got already and I'll take it from there."

Brock told Code what he knew about her personally then faxed him her résumé. When he hung up the phone, the image of Vanessa in that easy-to-undo sarong stayed on his mind.

Code wouldn't have anything to tell him until the morning at the very earliest, and Brock's patience had worn thin.

He stared at the phone for a second, then rose and headed back to the luau that was winding down. He had unfinished business with Vanessa that couldn't wait a second longer.

Vanessa stood at the shore watching the crushing waves die down to creep along the sand. Distant noise from the housekeeping crew taking tables and chairs away drifted in the air. With the tiki torches extinguished now, only a wide beam of moonlight lit the beach.

Vanessa rubbed her forehead, smoothing out throbbing tension that pounded in her skull. Sabotage had its drawbacks. She had worried herself sick over the luau and wondered how much longer Brock would tolerate her alleged mistakes. And she worried about Melody whom she hadn't spoken with in days. Her sister sent her vague text messages saying she's keeping busy trying to forget her heartache.

"Poor Melody," she whispered and another protective wave of motherly concern swept through her.

Brock's strong arms wrapped around her from behind and drew her back onto his chest. "Talking to yourself?"

Alarmed, Vanessa froze. Had he heard her call out Melody's name? He was too smart to fool much longer and she wasn't nearly through ruining him yet. She turned around and smiled, trying to read his expression. "Not really, just waiting for you."

Brock's brows rose, surprised. "The wait is over, baby."

Vanessa backed up a step. "I'm sorry about the luau."

Brock shook his head. "I'm not Brock, your boss, right now. It's after hours."

Vanessa was so relieved she thought she'd faint. She'd escaped her fate one more time. "Oh?"

"Take a walk with me."

Vanessa nodded and bent to remove her sandals. The minute she did, cool soft sand slipped between her toes. Brock entwined their fingers and they walked away from the luau area at Tranquility Bay.

"Being originally from Texas, I never had an appreciation for the ocean. But now, I can't imagine living anywhere else."

"Hawaii is a magical place," Vanessa agreed. She'd never seen such lush gardens or beautiful exotic flowers. The moment she stepped off the plane, she'd been pleasantly overtaken by the fragrant tropical scents that filled the air.

The night air grew cooler and she trembled. Brock noticed and put his arm around her, his large hand warming her bare shoulder. "Cold?"

"A little."

"How about a drink to warm you up?"

That sounded safe enough. They'd go to Joe's Tiki Torch just down the beach and be surrounded by people. Brock's sensuous touch always confused her. She had trouble remembering how much the cliché playboy millionaire had hurt her sister.

"That sounds nice. I could use a drink." That much wasn't a lie.

As they walked farther along the beach they passed the bar. Rock and roll music blasted out the doors. "Aren't we going in?" she asked, coming to a halt. She gestured toward the bar with her finger.

Brock shook his head, grabbed her pointed finger and tugged her along. "I have someplace better in mind. Where it's quiet."

When they reached the marina, Brock led her up the dock steps toward his yacht. Warning bells rang in her head. "On second thought, maybe I should just go home." She faked a yawn. "I'm tired."

Brock kept walking. "One drink, then I'll take you home if you want. I have something to discuss with you."

Uh-oh. Vanessa slammed her eyes shut. He would lower the boom now and maybe toss her overboard.

When she hesitated on the dock, he added, "It's important. Something personal." Then he smiled and she felt a wave of relief. Whatever Brock Tyler was, he wouldn't hurt her physically. He was a lady-killer in an entirely different fashion.

When they reached the *Rebecca,* Brock helped her board his boat and led her down the steps to a cozy sitting room. "It's warmer down here," he said. "Make yourself comfortable. I'll get you a drink."

Vanessa glanced at the large cushy sofa and opted to follow Brock to the bar. One drink. That's all she'd promised him. She watched him pour her a glass of plum wine while he poured himself something more toxic, whiskey straight up.

"So what did you want to discuss with me?" she asked, leaning on the bar. She held her breath hoping he wouldn't bring up the chaos at the luau.

Brock grimaced. "My mother's and brother's wedding. They're both getting married and want a double ceremony."

"How nice," she replied, thinking of mother and son sharing a wedding day. She'd bet that didn't happen too often.

"They want the wedding here, at Tempest Maui."

"Oh, well…that will be—"

"A nightmare if all doesn't go well. We can't have any mix-ups. I'm going to have to discuss the details with you tomorrow." He sipped his whiskey and a thoughtful expression crossed his features. "I want it to be perfect for them. We'll need to find a suitable date. They don't want to wait too long."

Vanessa kept silent.

He brought both of their drinks with him around the bar and handed her the plum wine. He touched his glass to hers in a toast. "Here's to things running smoothly from now on."

She forced a little smile and brought the glass up to her lips. "Of course." The sweet fruity wine slid down her throat, calming her fragile nerves a bit. She strolled over to the sliding glass door and looked out to the bay.

"Still cold?" he asked.

She shook her head. "The wine's warming me up. I'm fine now."

Brock opened the slider and sea air freshened the room. He faced her as a breeze blew a few strands of her hair onto her cheeks. She made a move to tuck those strands behind her ears. Brock gently took her wrist and lowered her hand down. "You look good windblown."

A chuckle escaped. "Really? Most women wouldn't consider that a compliment."

"You're not like most women."

She set her hands on her hips. "Now, I'm not sure that's a compliment either."

"Trust me. As a man who knows a lot about women, saying you're one of a kind is a compliment."

Vanessa sipped her drink and stared out the sliding door to the stars above. She felt things for Brock she had no business feeling. He drew her in and made her feel special. She hadn't had any luck with the opposite sex. She'd only known men who'd taken advantage of her. Brock was no different, she told herself over and over.

Until she looked deep into his eyes and saw someone quite *different.* Someone whose eyes gleamed with love when he spoke of his family. Someone who wanted to make his mother's and brother's wedding day special. Someone who was respected and considered a fair man by his employees.

Guilt set in. She was too close to the situation. She hadn't planned on getting personally involved with him. How could she? She was out to destroy him. For Melody and for herself.

Yes, she had to admit that she'd transferred some of her anger at the men who'd hurt her in the past onto Brock. She'd wanted him to pay, maybe not only for what he'd done to Melly, but for all the smug confident guys who'd disillusioned her in the past.

"I can't do this," she blurted. Surprised that she'd voiced her sentiments aloud, her eyes went wide and she took a step back.

"Don't go," Brock said, reaching for her. His hand slipped to the bow on her sarong. "Don't go," he said more softly, looking deeply into her eyes.

She moved her hand to his to halt him. The touch sparked electric currents that sizzled between them. She looked down at his strong capable hand, then gazed into his eyes again.

"Stay with me tonight."

It wasn't a command, but a request. His soft tone and the promise in his eyes tore away every shred of resistance she had inside.

*Oh, wow.*

She wanted to stay. More than she would have ever imagined. She dropped her hand to her side.

Brock blinked and slowly, effortlessly pulled the sash of her bow. She felt the material give and loosen, just like the clamp around her heart.

The material slid down her body, unraveling and dropping past her hips to puddle at her feet.

Brock gazed at her body, covered now with only a tiny black pair of panties. "My God," he said, blowing out a slow breath of appreciation. He shook his head, swallowed and continued to stare at her. "Come here, baby."

Vanessa hesitated a moment, recognizing the impact of what she was about to do. Unable to stop herself, she walked straight into Brock's arms.

# Seven

Brock brought his lips to hers and kissed her tenderly, reverently, taking his time. He caressed every inch of her he could reach and whispered his intent to drive her absolutely crazy tonight. Heat built quickly and she responded with little sounds of pleasure. She kissed him back fervently, locking her lips to his and then opening for more potent kisses. His tongue met with hers and the instant sensual connection heightened every sensation tenfold.

He took his time and drew out the pleasure, making her moan and sigh. Her nipples pebbled to tight buds. Moisture pooled at her pulsing core.

Still, Brock moved slowly, his hands working

magic, prickling her skin with jolt after jolt of dire intensity.

"I've wanted you. Be patient, Vanessa."

She'd never experienced anything so powerful in her life. She wanted him inside her, claiming her, making her feel like a desired woman. It'd been so long since she'd felt anything remotely like this. Her heart pounded in her ears. Her entire body shook with need. She gave in to Brock, surrendering her body and soul to him.

It felt right.

And honest.

That was a joke, since she'd lied to him over and over. Nothing about the two of them was honest. But this…*this,* was something she'd dreamed about only in her secret, most private fantasies.

He moved down to suckle her breast with his mouth, the palm of one hand rubbing the tip of her nipple, the other teasing the dampest spot between her legs. She moaned softly, the pleasure about to burst her wide open. "Please, Brock," she breathed out.

"I know, baby. I know." He broke off his kisses and looked into her eyes.

Raw desire, a potent hunger she'd never seen before, reflected back at her. Her heart beat feverishly and her desire for him escalated even more.

He lifted her in one smooth move and she clung to him. He walked briskly past the galley to the master suite. There, he set her down on the big masculine-looking bed and instead of joining her he took a step back. “I’ve pictured you here a dozen times. But the real thing,” he said, with true awe in his voice, “the real thing is staggering, Vanessa.”

Vanessa closed her eyes. She couldn’t believe where she was. She couldn’t believe who she was with. But it didn’t matter. None of it. Not anymore. She wanted Brock Tyler and tonight her mind and body focused on only one thing.

She smiled as she watched him take off his shoes. A real man knew that’s where you started to undress for a lady. Next, he tore at the buttons of his shirt. She took a deep breath, fully inspired by his broad chest, the ripples of muscles that weren’t overkill, but just perfect. The zipper came down slowly and she witnessed him in full form finally, his silky manhood erect.

Her throat constricted. If it were humanly possible she was even more aroused than before.

He covered himself with protection and instead of coming down to her, he reached for her hand and lifted her off the bed. When she stood, he kissed her, crushing his mouth to hers in a lusty display of heated passion. Then he lifted her slight form up, holding her buttocks. “Hang on to me,” he rasped out and she draped her arms around his neck tight and wrapped her legs around his waist.

“Oh, wow,” she whispered, breathless. Then the tip of his manhood nudged inside her, teasing her with his full erection.

“Okay, baby?”

She bit her lip from screaming yes, yes, yes and nodded.

Holding her carefully, he drove himself deep, filling her full, guiding her with his hands until she learned his pace. Then she moved on him, gyrating her body, the grind and drawback inching her closer and closer to ecstasy.

Brock kissed her hard on the lips, moving with her as she took him inside deeper and deeper.

When they were both on the edge of completion, Brock lowered her down onto his bed and struck the last potent chord, arching up and groaning along with her raspy moans of intense pleasure.

She came first, her explosion stunning her. She bent her body upwards and took all Brock had to give. She shattered completely, Brock only seconds behind.

He dropped onto her and kissed her soundly before rolling next to her, his arm wrapped tightly around her shoulder.

"Wow," she said, curling up to him.

He hugged her close and kissed the top of her head. "You could say that."

"I do keep saying that, don't I?" She was blissfully happy.

"I plan to keep you saying that."

She nibbled on her lower lip, hardly containing her joy. "Really?"

Brock turned onto his side to look into her eyes. God how he hoped his suspicions about her were unfounded. He had good instincts, but he'd been mistaken before. This was one time he hoped he'd been paranoid and dead wrong. This was one time he hoped his instincts failed him.

Vanessa was the woman he wanted in his life right now. No other woman had intrigued him like this. He'd fallen deeply in lust with her.

He glanced at her pillow and noticed the lavender orchid that had adorned her hair. He picked it up and twirled it around in his fingers, staring at it. The flower reminded him of her—soft and delicate but firm to the touch and more resilient than it looked. He positioned the flower behind her left ear then gazed into her blue eyes. "Consider yourself *taken* from now on, Vanessa."

She brought her chin up. "Don't I have a say in this?" she asked, but her soft sweet tone belied the sincerity of her question.

He caressed her arm, sliding his hand up to her shoulder. "Of course. You can agree," he said. "Or I can spend the rest of the night convincing you."

There was no doubt in his mind he'd make love to her again tonight.

Vanessa blinked and then roped her arms around him. "I'm not easily convinced."

Brock smiled and kissed her lips gently. "I was hoping you'd say that."

Brock was an insatiable lover. After an hour of soft whispers and tempting foreplay, he made love to her again. With patience this time, he explored her body and made her aware of her femininity as no man had ever before. Vanessa relished the night hours she spent in his arms. She relished the way he kissed her and touched her, making sure she was completely satisfied before taking his pleasure. She drifted in and out of sleep, waking every few hours to find herself beside him, cradled in his strong arms.

In the morning, sunlight reflected onto the blue marina waters and beamed brightly into the bedroom, waking her. She savored the warmth a second and squinted her eyes open. She found Brock watching her, his body turned her way, his head propped on his hand.

"Morning," he said with a quick smile.

"Hi." She felt suddenly shy, remembering the night they'd shared together. She'd been almost as insatiable as Brock. Images of erotic positions and lusty words spoken stirred in her mind. "Am I really here with you?"

Brock caressed her arm, then lowered his hand to fondle her breast. "You're here, baby. Making all my fantasies come true."

"All?" His touch sent her mind spinning again.

He leaned forward and kissed her gently. "Maybe not *all.* I have a few left in store for you."

"Such as?"

When had she gotten so brazen? Maybe it all started when she'd found Melody crying hysterically about the man who'd broken her heart. Maybe that's when

Vanessa had become this bold, gutsy woman who'd flown halfway across the world to get revenge.

Brock yanked their sheets off. He clasped her hand and lifted her from the bed. "Want to find out?"

She did. She really wasn't ready for this to end. She'd admonish herself later for sleeping with the enemy. And wouldn't think of the complications last night would impose on her plans. Right now she'd entertain her own fantasies and deal with the consequences later. Right now she'd be selfish and take what she wanted from this man.

"Yes. Show me."

Without hesitation, Brock led her to the small enclave in the room that housed the yacht's shower. He turned the water on. "Ready to get wet and wild?"

She roped her arms around him and pressed every inch of her body to his. "Maybe I already am."

He growled, low and deep in his throat and stepped in, pulling her with him. The brass faucet spit out bursts of hot spray that hit their bodies with prickling force. Stimulating rain aroused as much as it refreshed.

Brock picked up a bar of soap and rubbed it between his palms, creating a handful of rich bubbly lather. He coated her shoulders with the lather and worked his magic, rubbing her skin and smoothing his hands over her with strong capable strokes. Next, his hands rounded over her breasts, circling and cupping them, his fingertips dragging across her nipples, teasing, tempting.

"Brock," she pleaded. She was already consumed with enough heat to explode.

She thought she'd hate herself in the morning for the sexual indulgence she allowed herself last night. But it *was* morning now and she didn't hate herself at all. No, she only wanted more from Brock.

Was something wrong with her?

Had she been so sexually deprived these last few years that she'd had to resort to making love with the one man on earth she shouldn't? Or, was Brock so damned good in bed that he made her lose her head last night?

And quite possibly her heart.

*Don't fall for him, Vanessa.*

The thought was obliterated when he crushed his lips to hers. His potent kiss fueled a fire in her belly and brought her back into the moment. He continued to lather her body, turning her around, running his fingers along her spine and then palming her cheeks.

She felt his powerful erection nudge her and she whipped around, smiling. "Not yet."

He looked at her quizzically when she took up the bar of soap and built up lather. Next, she lathered him up, running her hands down his chest and below his navel. She heard his soft intake of breath, which gave her the courage to go on. Splaying her fingers wide, she cupped his shaft and stroked over him sliding her hand around his male organ.

He grinned. "I like the way you think."

But his smile was short-lived when her stroking became more intense. He closed his eyes and leaned back against the shower stall, enjoying the pleasure she created. It did her heart good to hear his stirring groans of enjoyment.

When she stopped, he snapped his eyes open.

"Can you guess what I'm thinking now?" she asked.

He drew in oxygen. "I can only hope, baby."

She maneuvered herself onto her knees and sat back across her legs. Next, she cupped his manhood and drew him deep into her mouth.

He held his breath, and when she moved on him he cursed explicitly, giving up all control and power. She accepted the role as aggressor and enjoyed every second of making love to him this way. When she brought him to the height of pleasure, he halted her and lifted her up. "Can't take another second," he admitted, his expression one of fierce restraint.

He kissed her with open-mouthed frenzy and things got wild after that. Brock parted her legs and palmed her womanhood until she thought she'd go mad. Her body hummed, her skin prickled, steamy water showered her and she thought she'd burn up inside.

He brought his mouth to her parted thighs and stroked her with his tongue until she nearly cried out her climax, but she held back. "Now, Brock. Now."

He rose quickly, wrapped her legs around his waist and entered her, both were fiery hot and ready to climb to the ultimate peak together. His thrusts were sure and hard and fast. The pleasure erotic, Vanessa had never in her life been loved so thoroughly.

They climaxed together, making pleas and grunts in unison until both exploded with earth-shattering potency.

Brock shut the shower off. He wrapped his arms around her and held her there for long minutes, kissing her hair, murmuring soft exquisite words, tucking her into the safety of his body. They stood that way until a chill overtook their sated wet bodies.

Then Brock wrapped her in a big lush towel and carried her to the bed. He set her down and laid down next to her, cradling her tight. "Sleep now, baby. We both need it."

She drifted off in his arms, praying to God she hadn't just made the biggest mistake of her life.

"Melly, calm down, honey. Please stop crying." As she sat on her sofa, kicking her sandals off, Vanessa's stomach tightened with a sick ache as she listened to Melody's sad disheartened sobs. Vanessa had hoped that her sister had moved on somewhat from her heartache. But Melody had always been impetuous and spirited. Her emotions ran high. When she was up, no one on earth was happier, but when she was down, unfortunately, she felt keen despair.

"Okay, Vanny," she said, stifling her sobs. "I'll…try to stop. Sorry, I didn't mean to break down like that. It's good to hear your voice." She sounded more composed now, to Vanessa's relief. "It's just been a hard week for me."

"Still thinking of…*him?*"

"Oh, yes," Melody rushed out. "*Always.*"

Vanessa snapped her eyes shut. Dear Lord. She felt like Benedict Arnold. Why had she allowed Brock Tyler to charm and seduce her last night? "Would it do any good to say that he's not worth it?"

"Oh, Vanny. He is. He is *so* worth it. You just don't know."

She did know. That was the problem. She'd just spent an entire night with him. And for a few hours, Vanessa had been caught up in a whirlwind of desire. Her mind had clouded, fogged up completely by a handsome face, a commanding male body and just the right words spoken. She'd forgotten who Brock Tyler really was and had been foolish enough to believe she'd been wrong about him. Secretly, she'd wanted out of her self-imposed mission to cause him pain and ruin his reputation.

Vanessa knocked herself upside the head mentally and pounded some sense into her brain. She told herself the last twenty-four hours were a bad dream.

The reality hit her hard.

She'd slept with the man responsible for causing her baby sister's terrible grief and heartache.

"Vanessa, you're a dope," she whispered.

"What?" Melody asked on a shaky breath.

"Nothing, honey. I'm sorry. I wish I could give you a big hug."

"Me, too. I could use it."

"Really? I mean, I can quit my job and come home, Melly. I would. I'd do that."

"Don't be silly, Van," she said on a sniffle. "You *can't* quit your job."

Oh, but Vanessa wanted to. She wanted out of this place, away from Brock Tyler, who'd done nothing but confuse and confound her. She was certain he was a master at seduction. A true devil in disguise.

"I'll be fine…really," Melody said on a shaky breath.

"You're sure?"

"Yes, I've just had a hard, stressful week. Tanya is taking me to see a movie tonight. It'll get my mind off…things."

Vanessa sucked oxygen into her lungs, grateful her sister had her best friend there to hold her hand and keep her company. If Vanessa couldn't be there, then Tanya was surely a great replacement. "That's good, honey. And work is going okay?"

"Work? Sure. The shop's picking up and I'm doing decent business."

Melody ran the gift shop in the hotel that was independently owned from Tempest New Orleans. She'd started her own business and had an eye for unique items that couldn't be found in local Louisiana venues. Melly was good with people, friendly, outgoing and genuine. Those traits probably caught Brock's eye and he'd taken advantage of her without so much as a drop of remorse.

"Well, I'm glad I reached you. You've been hard to track down," Vanessa said. "I guess I worry too much about my baby sister."

"I'm sorry. I've been, uh, like I said, it's been a stressful week."

"Just try not to think about Brock anymore, Melly."

"Brock?" Melody paused and Vanessa cursed silently. She shouldn't have brought up his name. "Oh…um, I'll try not to."

"Okay. That's a start. Give Mom a kiss for me. You *are* visiting her, aren't you?"

"I haven't missed a Sunday."

Sweeping sadness washed over her. Ten years ago, their mother had been a victim of a hit and run accident. She'd never really recovered from the physical trauma and the doctors believed it had caused her early-onset Alzheimer's disease. Luckily, their mom still knew them, but she couldn't function as a parent. While Vanessa's father had died recently, Melody's father had walked out after the accident, unable to deal with the drastic changes in their lives. Vanessa had taken over the role as parent and had mothered Melody ever since.

She couldn't help the fierce protectiveness she felt for her sister. Melody had always needed nurturing. She'd always needed to feel loved. Brock's sudden and coldhearted dismissal of her had broken her heart in the same way her father's abandonment had.

How could she have forgotten that? How had she allowed her attraction to him sway her resolve?

Vanessa said goodbye to Melody then clicked off the phone, admonishing herself for being vulnerable. She'd allowed herself one blissful night with a dangerously tempting man and now self-loathing and guilt consumed her. She'd made a slip, a false move by sleeping with Brock, but now she was back on track.

She wouldn't falter again.

Nothing would deter her.

Vanessa dressed for work quickly, her mind spinning, her thoughts keyed in on the best way to accomplish her goal.

She left her condo with a plan in mind to sabotage the next big hotel event and it was nothing short of genius.

Brock slammed down his office phone and stared at it for a long drawn-out minute, as if the damn thing would rectify the words he'd just heard come across the wire from Code Landon.

Her sister runs the gift shop at Tempest New Orleans. You dated her a while back. Melody Applegate. The two are very close.

Brock couldn't believe it. Though he'd suspected something was up, he hadn't wanted to believe it. He hadn't wanted to believe the most exciting woman he'd met since he'd stolen a kiss from luscious Serena Barton in high school, wasn't whom he thought she was.

No, he'd thought Vanessa Dupree was one of a kind.

Hell, he sure got that right.

"Damn you, Vanessa."

Brock pushed away from his desk and rose from his chair. He paced the floor glaring at the phone, going over and over every memory he had of Melody Applegate. Sure, they'd dated. For about a month. She was a sweet kid. Too sweet and young for him, he'd determined.

There hadn't been any sparks at all. He'd let her down gently once he realized that they hadn't a thing in common.

And then he remembered one other important thing about Melody Applegate.

His mind turned to Vanessa. She'd known all along. She had to. She wouldn't speak of her sister, only letting it slip once that she even had a sibling.

Brock turned black with anger. He fisted and unfisted his hands. His gut clenched and his mind ran rampant. Vanessa had been behind the disasters at the hotel. It had to be. She held some sort of depraved vendetta against him. That had to be the reason she'd been so hard to seduce. She'd been out to ruin his hotel and she'd been clever, covering her tracks so that nothing she did could be proven.

Brock strode to the wet bar and hastily poured himself a drink of whiskey straight up. The liquid splashed out the tumbler and he cursed. At the mess.

At Vanessa Dupree. At her lies and her deception. At her clever taunts and the way she'd suckered him in.

No one made a fool of Brock Tyler.

No one.

Brock gulped a swig of whiskey and strode to the balcony. Outside, all looked peaceful. The sun shone bright against the crystal aqua ocean waters. He thought of Vanessa, her eyes matching the hues of the Pacific. Just last night she'd fulfilled his fantasies. She'd been a willing, eager participant and they'd rocked that boat until sunrise. Sexy, gorgeous, erotic, she'd been everything he'd imagined and more. They had heat together and combusted into flames like two sticks of dynamite.

She'd been the one woman he'd wanted above all else.

Anger, raw and fresh, registered in what she'd just thrown away.

He gulped whiskey with a solemn vow. "I'm going to fire your ass, Vanessa Dupree."

Then a thought struck. Firing her wasn't good enough. She deserved more than that for trying to take him down. She deserved much worse.

Brock contemplated for twenty minutes, tamping down bitter disappointment and anger. He finished his drink. When his nerves calmed, he buzzed his secretary. "Send for Akamu. I need a meeting with him right away."

His hotel manager walked in a few minutes later and Brock looked him dead in the eye. "What I'm about to tell you can't go any farther than this room."

Akamu nodded, his usual big smile tucked away. He knew when Brock meant business. Yet he couldn't conceal a wide-eyed look of astonishment when Brock laid out all the facts.

"You're sure it's Vanessa?" he asked.

Brock drew in a breath, then sighed. "I'm sure. Do I have your loyalty?"

"Always."

"I'll expect daily reports from you."

Akamu nodded.

Brock went on. "I know she's your friend. This can't be easy for you, but I need to know you're looking out for the best interests of the hotel."

A thoughtful look crossed his expression and his dark eyes narrowed. "The hotel is my top priority. It's a good plan, boss. I'll do my best."

Brock smiled at the Hawaiian. "Good." Then Brock added curiously, "I thought you liked Vanessa?"

. "Everyone likes Vanessa." Then he shrugged and shook his head contemplating. "I keep my business separate from my personal life."

Brock set his stance and looked out at the tranquil bay, crushing down regret that threatened to tear him up. "That's probably wise, Akamu."

He should have done that. Kept his business separate from his pleasure. But Vanessa had turned his head. And the most skeptical part of him wondered if she'd deliberately set out to keep him distracted by tempting and teasing him. She'd managed to blindside him. But never again.

The woman couldn't be trusted.

Brock resigned himself to what he had to do. At least playing cat and mouse with the wily woman would keep him entertained while he served up his retaliation. He wasn't through with Vanessa Dupree.

Not by a long shot.

There wasn't much Vanessa could do about Sunday evening's luau. After the fiasco on Saturday night with Brock in attendance patching up the chaos she'd caused, she couldn't chance another misstep so soon. She'd gotten away with it and forged forward to do more damage.

Besides, she hadn't the mind for it on Sunday. No, she'd been too busy with Brock that morning. On his boat. Making love to him.

Oh, man.

She'd really blown it.

Vanessa shook off thoughts of his stunning ripped body. His handsome face. His erotic words while he made love to her.

She turned her thoughts to her next plan of action. It was brilliant even if she did say so herself. After all, she couldn't confide in anyone, not a soul, so she commended herself with a mental pat on the back for her clever plan.

The midweek miniconferences held in spacious

ballrooms were big moneymakers for the hotel. The rooms were rented out for lectures and workshops. The hotel made money on guest charges, rental space and meals served. Hundreds of paid guests spent their money in the gift shops, bars and poolside as well.

Vanessa made the last and final phone call to secure all was right on track and sat back at her desk with smug satisfaction.

"A.R.M. meets Lily's Designs," she whispered with a smile. "It's better than Frankenstein meets the Wolfman."

"Talking to yourself again, Vanessa?" Brock stood at the threshold of her office.

"Uh, a bad habit of mine," she said. Then gulped. She hadn't seen Brock in the office, or anywhere for that matter, for three days.

He'd called her house and left a sweet message every day apologizing for his busy schedule. She'd been home, listening, screening the calls and staring at the phone, debating whether to pick it up. What would she say to him? How would she react? The coward in her won out and she'd let her answering machine accept all of her calls, avoiding him. Which was ridiculous since she knew they'd have to come face-to-face eventually.

"Did you get the flowers I sent?"

Vanessa rose from her desk and straightened out her black-and-white-print dress. Mustering bravado, she smiled. "Yes, they were lovely. Thank you."

Brock walked into her office and closed the door behind him.

Vanessa worried her lip, sucking in oxygen.

Brock looked good. He wore white trousers and a russet shirt that set off his tanned skin. Her heart dipped a little. But she picked it right back up, determined to stay the course. The gleam she witnessed in his eyes told her he had other plans.

"I've missed you," he said, coming to stand before her.

She blinked. "You missed me?"

"In my bed, Vanessa. You do remember how it was between us," he rasped in a low voice, his gaze leveled on hers.

Staggered by his bluntness, she fumbled for the right words. "Oh…yes," she said breathlessly, not at all how she'd intended to respond.

Brock grinned, his eyes darkened with intensity. "I don't think I've had a better night in my life." He moved closer. "How about you?"

She backed up. "Me?"

He came forward and lifted a strand of her hair, studying it. "I think I counted four orgasms, Vanessa." His gaze found hers again. Rapid heat sizzled between them. "Does that qualify for a great night with you?"

Vanessa squeezed her eyes shut momentarily, reminded of her wanton behavior and her intense physical enjoyment that night. "It was wonderful." She couldn't lie about that. She wasn't that much of a fraud.

"Good, I hope you aren't the kind of woman who'd say it was a mistake. That nonsense doesn't fly after spending the entire night naked together, doing the things we did to each other."

"Oh, um." What did he expect her to say to that?

It had been a mistake. *A big mistake.* And more importantly, there would be no repeat performances. But a tiny part of her wondered what Brock would do for an encore if they were to get together again.

Brock leaned in. Vanessa backed up again. This time the back of her legs hit the edge of her desk. She was as far as she could go, in many ways.

Brock closed the gap between them. His stance spread wide, encasing her body. He took hold of her waist and tugged her to him, splaying his hands on her backside. The second he touched her, sensations swept through her with shocking force. Her body reacted. She hated that it did. She stared at his shirt, opened at the throat and remembered gliding her tongue over that very spot.

"What's the matter, Vanessa?" he asked.

"I'm swamped. Feeling distracted at the moment," she said. "You caught me by surprise."

"I caught you talking to yourself. You didn't look busy."

"Trust me. I'm busy."

Brock hesitated a moment, then released her. He glanced at the papers on her desk. Walking around the desk, he picked up a manila folder and studied the cover. "Working on the A.R.M. account?"

Vanessa reached for the file and tugged it out of his hand. "Yes. It's coming up in less than a week." Without looking at the folder, she tucked it away quickly in her drawer, her heart hammering, worried she might have made some notes that were for her eyes only.

Brock walked over to the window in her office and looked out. "I'm fond of animals myself. What about you?"

She nodded. "Love them."

He turned. "So, you're an advocate for the Animal Rights March?"

She tilted her head and became thoughtful. "They can be a little extreme at times. But I'm all for kindness to animals."

"You should see my brother Trent's place in Crimson Canyon. He's got a herd of wild horses on his property. It's a sight to behold."

Vanessa remained silent. Brock seemed reflective at the moment and she was grateful he'd focused his attention on something other than her.

"That's why I'm here, Vanessa. To talk about Trent's wedding. And my mother's. We need to find a date that's doable for everyone."

"Oh, I'll be happy to do that."

Brock nodded and studied her a moment. "The luau went smoothly on Sunday. I'm pleased with the results. I think we may have ironed out all of our problems."

The luau went well only because she'd been in bed with him when she should have been plotting another minicatastrophe. She returned the nod. "Me, too."

Brock walked over to her and cupped her face in his hands. Before she could react, he brushed his lips over hers gently, kissing her with tenderness. "Check your calendar and get back to me with those dates."

He left her, staggered by the impact of that kiss.

And wishing he was anyone but Brock Elliot Tyler, her sworn enemy.

# Eight

The next day, Akamu walked into Brock's office, a file folder tucked under his right arm. Brock gestured for the hotel manager to sit down across from him. "I take it you have some information for me?"

"Boy, do I. Starting Monday we have five scheduled conferences booked for the week. One that's an all-day event, three that are two-day events and," he said, opening his file and checking, "one that goes for three full days."

"Should bring the hotel revenue up. Can we accommodate that many?"

"It'll be tight, boss. We've never had so many booked in one week before. All the meeting rooms will be holding events."

Brock contemplated. “Any other news?”

Akamu grinned, then caught himself and soured his expression. “If you’re asking about Vanessa, yes. I have news. I know what she’s up to.”

Brock took a deep breath. A small part of him held some hope that he’d been wrong about the blond bombshell with brains. Akamu’s admission now slashed that hope. “What news?”

Again, Akamu’s mouth quirked up before he spoke and his expression took on a look of respect. “She planned the Long A.R.M. for Justice meeting in the Melia Room. And Lily’s Designs sales meeting in the Loke Lau Room.”

“Those rooms face each other. Now explain.” Brock leaned against the back of his chair and steepled his fingers, waiting.

Akamu didn’t attempt to hide his admiration. “You know what A.R.M. stands for, right?”

“Only a hermit living in the Sahara Desert wouldn’t know A.R.M. They’re a very vocal group.”

“Animal activists,” Akamu said.

“Go on.”

“Lily’s Designs specializes in selling designer handbags and accessories made exclusively with fur and leather. Seems our event planner has made a deal with Lily herself to showcase some of her top-selling designs in glass cases just outside the ballroom where her sales meeting takes place.”

“Hell! Vanessa will rub A.R.M.’s nose in it.”

Akamu bobbed his head in acknowledgment. "It's brilliant."

Brock glared at him, frowning at Vanessa's deceit and Akamu immediately cleared his throat and shifted in his seat nervously.

"Brilliant," Brock droned between tight lips. "They'll have a volcanic shouting match at best."

"Or, they might come to blows. I've seen it a few times on late-night news. One of these activists sees a fur coat and they go *pupule*." He circled his index finger around his temple a few times.

Brock rubbed his forehead. He'd seen the craziness, too. Red wine splashed across a fur coat. Riots in the streets. Celebrities rising up to the A.R.M. cause. "Is she planning anything else?"

Akamu shook his head. "I don't think so. I've been over everything a dozen times."

"No, she probably thought this would be enough. There's no need for icing on the cake. She's probably thinking this was a sweet enough deal."

Akamu remained silent.

Brock thought on this awhile and then leaned in, lowering his voice. "Okay, I have a plan. Here's what will happen next."

Twenty minutes later, satisfied that his plan would work and his reputation would be salvaged, at least this week, Brock walked the distance to Vanessa's office.

* * *

"Darn it, Melody. Why don't you answer your phone?" She stared at the screen for a second, wondering why her sister was so hard to contact. She'd been checking in with her every other day leaving voice mail messages. Most of the time Vanessa only got brief text messages back from her.

Vanessa slipped her cell phone back into her little pink leather purse she'd bought at a discount, a knockoff of one of Lily's classic designs. She couldn't afford the real thing. Those designer handbags went for a small fortune. Her mind clicked forward to the little fiasco waiting to happen on Monday. What a way to kick off the week.

"I need a word with you." Brock Tyler appeared at her door. His eyes, deep, dark and deliciously brown, honed in on her.

She gasped. She had to be more careful. Brock was one to simply show up unannounced. Not that he hadn't a perfect right—he was the owner of the hotel and her employer. She did answer to him, on one level.

"Hi!" She sounded a little too glad to see him. Overcompensating had always been a flaw of hers.

She must have given him the wrong impression because he closed the door behind him and strode over to her desk. She kept her eyes on him as he bent down and kissed her soundly on the lips until her nipples puckered under her blouse. He nuzzled her neck a second and she drank in his familiar scent. "Hi, back at you, baby."

Vanessa chewed on her lip. "You wanted to see me?"

Brock's grin was pure sin. "Always."

Heat crawled up her throat. With just a look he could make her squirm. She hated that about him. He was like a force of nature, a windstorm that pulled you in the wrong direction.

Lucy opened the door and popped her head in. "Hey, how about lunch today," she blurted before realizing Vanessa had company. "Oops! Sorry, Mr. Tyler."

Brock backed away from Vanessa and smiled at Lucy. "Not a problem."

"I'll come back later."

Thank God for Lucy. She had good timing, Vanessa thought. "Lunch sounds good, Lucy," she managed to call out before Lucy shut the door, her footsteps fading down the hallway.

Vanessa gathered up files on her desk and set them in neat little piles. She inhaled, aware of Brock's eyes on her.

"I won't keep you from lunch," he said. "Just wanted to get back to you about the date."

"The *date?*" Vanessa's mind raced. Had she made a date with him?

"For the double wedding."

"Oh." Was that disappointment she felt? She'd spent one erotic night with Brock and he'd only made half-hearted attempts to see her again. Her ego was bruised in one respect but in another she was grateful that she didn't have to come up with excuses to refuse him.

He pointed to the calendar on her desk. "This day works good for everyone."

Vanessa glanced down at the calendar to where his finger had landed. "That's less than three weeks away!"

"Are you saying it's not doable?" He pinned her down with a curious look.

"Well, um." She'd given him dates that were available last night, but she'd never dreamed that they'd take the earliest possible one. Vanessa didn't want to be working at Tempest when his family arrived. She didn't want any part of their wedding. "It's gonna be a push to get everything perfect."

"I have faith in you. You're more than capable of pulling this off."

Vanessa looked away momentarily, chewing a little harder on her lip. He trusted her to make his mother's and brother's joint wedding perfect. Vanessa's resolve dipped to a new low. Ruining his family's wedding would put her in a reptilian class of creatures. "Sure, I can pull it off. But maybe *they* need a little more time."

"Mom's been alone most of her life. She and Matthew don't want to wait any longer. And Trent doesn't have a patient bone in his body."

"Well, okay. I'll see what I can do."

She caught Brock's quick frown before he nodded. "Consider it a personal favor to me."

Vanessa didn't want to do Brock any favors.

"Lucy will help you with anything you need."

Oh, great. Now Lucy was involved. "Wonderful."

"Thank you." Brock braced his hands on her desk and leaned in. He smiled and touched a finger to her cheek, the soft caress gliding down to her mouth. He traced her lips tenderly and she caught the potent yet subtle hint of his sandalwood scent. He brought his mouth down gently. The sweetness of his slow kiss rippled through her heart.

"Have a nice lunch, Vanessa."

She snapped her eyes open and found him staring at her with an odd expression. Just a glimpse, a second in time, she noticed vulnerability on Brock's face before he turned and walked out of her office.

He left her shattered and confused. Vanessa crossed her hands over her chest and slumped in her seat fighting the question that had begun to plague her constantly. Was it possible to hate someone and love them at the same time?

She feared she knew the answer, because a heart didn't lie.

It was worth the cost of Tempest Maui itself, to see the bewildered look on Vanessa's face Monday morning when she walked down the hallway to the bank of meeting rooms that in no way resembled the chaos she'd originally planned. Her gaze darted from one meeting room to the other and finally settled on the construction blockades in front of the Melia Room.

"What happened to the Animal Rights March group?" she probed Akamu.

Brock stood in an alcove, out of sight, listening and sneaking a peek at her discourse with his hotel manager.

"I had them scheduled in the Melia Room. The room should've been set up by now."

Akamu replied, "A pipe burst in that room last night. Water soaked the carpets. The whole place reeks. Mold. Yuck." Akamu pinched his nose. "You wouldn't want to go in there."

"Why wasn't I notified?" Vanessa asked. Brock smiled hearing her ire rise.

"Oh, no need to wake you up. It happened very very late last night."

Vanessa paced and narrowed her eyes as a crew set up the Loke Lau Room for Lily's Designs. Lily's employees worked diligently, placing handbags and accessories on display tables, the smell of new leather strong.

"What on earth did you do with the animal group?"

"A brainstorm," Akamu answered. "The Atrium Restaurant is available today on the top floor. It's being set up as we speak and I'm sure the president of the group will be glad to hear they'll have such a beautiful room for their conference."

"They don't know?"

"No, I thought you should call him. You're good with smoothing things out. Here," he said, punching in the number and handing her his cell phone. "Be sure to tell them we have natural exhibits up there and a waterfall. They'll have no complaints. The room is ready for them."

Vanessa's lips curved down as she took the phone from his hand. "Right. But you should have called me about this."

Akamu shrugged, ignoring her irritation.

Brock waited until she finished her phone conversation to walk up to them, enjoying every second of Vanessa's discomfort. He glanced around the bank of meeting rooms, making a point to note the construction blockades. "Problems?" he asked.

Akamu launched into the story, finishing with, "And Vanessa just called the president of A.R.M. to tell them they'll have their conference today in the Atrium Restaurant. She set it all up."

"Is that true? They're okay with it?"

Vanessa nodded. "Yes, they seemed pleased when I explained the amenities in the Atrium. They won't have a moment of delay. Their conference will start as scheduled."

"Good thinking, Vanessa," Brock said. "You averted a disaster."

"But it was Akamu's idea," she blurted.

Akamu nudged her. "Vanessa is too modest. She's the charmer. She could sell sand to a beach bum."

"Good job." Brock glanced at Vanessa, whose smile was reluctant at best. "Both of you."

Akamu looked at his watch, then excused himself.

Vanessa started to retreat as well. "I'd better get back to—"

"Just a minute, Vanessa," he said, reaching for her arm. He slipped his hand down to her slight wrist then took her hand. "I want to talk to you."

The beautiful deceiver stiffened and fear entered her eyes. Brock enjoyed her moment of guilt. He led her to the alcove he'd ducked into minutes ago. With her back to the wall, she blinked and refused to look him in the eyes. "What?"

He tipped her chin up and forced her to meet his gaze. "This."

He met with the softness of her mouth and kissed her until her tension faded. He wanted her still, even though he knew she was out to destroy him. Even through all the deceit. Brock wasn't going to forgive her. He wouldn't let her off the hook. But he wasn't immune to her charms.

She was an addiction.

And a challenge.

Now that Brock knew what he was dealing with, he'd watch his back, cover his bases, but wouldn't deny himself the pleasurable benefits Vanessa could provide.

No way would he let her have anything to do with his mother's and brother's wedding. He didn't trust her. But she didn't know that and he had to keep her thinking that he was clueless.

Until he tired of the game.

"Brock," she huffed out, breathless.

He searched her deviously gorgeous blue eyes. "What?" he whispered, trailing kisses along her throat. She arched her back instinctively; the erotic move jarred him and he groaned. "Damn it, Vanessa."

She had him hot and ready in a flash. He had to control his animal instincts or he'd be dropping her to the floor, right there in the middle of his hotel. He backed away from her and she opened eyes filled with the same hunger as his.

"Brock," she murmured, repeating his name. Her voice sounded small and vulnerable this time. Tears filled her eyes. Confusion marred her expression. She shook her head and brushed past him in a flurry, her high heels scraping the marble floor as she raced to get away.

Stunned, Brock watched her leave, his stomach knotting up and gutted inside.

She deserves this, he told himself.

But he walked back to his office without feeling one true ounce of satisfaction.

Joe's Tiki Torch was less crowded than usual for hump Wednesday, yet the music blared as if people were packed in wall to wall. Vanessa sat at a small corner table facing her piña colada and her friend Lucy.

"You didn't eat much at dinner, now you're not drinking. What's up?" Lucy asked, with kindness in her eyes.

She really was a dear friend, not the frivolous kind that would dump you at the first of sign of trouble, or worse yet, relish your particular anguish. No, Lucy was true blue.

Which made Vanessa feel terrible about what she'd been trying to do. Pangs of guilt plagued her lately. She'd set out to destroy Brock in his newly renovated hotel, but she'd never contemplated making friends here, ones she cared about dearly.

Lucy was a gem.

Akamu had come through like a trooper and a loyal friend on Monday. He'd covered for her and taken care of the conference fiasco on his own—then generously gave her full credit for fixing the very problem she'd tried to create.

She sighed, plucked out the yellow flowered umbrella from the tall colada glass and took a sip. She couldn't believe her rotten luck. Who would think a water pipe bursting would actually save Brock's butt?

"I'm a little down tonight. Sorry if I'm bad company," she said to Lucy.

"That's why we're here. To cheer you up! You've been like this since Monday."

Lucy had asked her several times in the past few days what was wrong and Vanessa had made up one excuse after another. What could she say? *I'm falling in love with the man I'm planning on destroying? If I succeed, your job might be in jeopardy.*

She reminded herself to think of all the Melodys in

the world who'd been hurt badly by men like Brock. She reminded herself how hard she'd tried to be both mother and father to Melly these past years. She'd protected her from fickle girlfriends, teachers who'd been unfair and cagey young men who weren't good enough for her. She'd taught her how to drive defensively and how to dance. She'd helped her with her high school prom and college sorority events. She'd always been there for Melody, her baby sister.

"I'll lighten up." She smiled for Lucy and sipped her drink again. The pineapple, coconut and rum slid down her throat like an alcoholic milk shake. "This isn't half bad."

Lucy narrowed her dark eyes and nodded. "You can tell me anything, you know."

"I know." But she couldn't tell her *this*.

Vanessa was asked to dance a few times and each time, with Lucy's prodding, she got up and danced. Lucy was a free spirit. She lost herself in dance, laughing and moving around the dance floor with her partners without a care in the world.

Vanessa really tried to lighten up. She wanted to have fun, but lately she felt like a stick in the mud. She'd refused an offer to go outside and get some air and another blatant offer to see her dance partner's own *tiki torch.*

She sat down, winded, looking at her watch and wishing she'd driven her own car to the bar. Those thoughts were quadrupled when Brock walked into the

Torch with Larissa Montrayne, the woman who'd monopolized all of Brock's time the other night. Supposedly, she was engaged to be married, but one wouldn't know it by the way she clung to Brock's arm. They strode up to the bar, their backs to her.

Vanessa turned away from them, wishing she could escape out the back door. She met with Lucy's questioning stare instead. "You look like a tiger ready to pounce."

Vanessa clenched her teeth. "No, I don't. I'm fine." She plastered on a fake smile.

"You don't look fine." Lucy looked around the entire room and stopped when she spotted Brock with Larissa at the bar. She cast Vanessa a sympathetic look. "Oh, I get it now."

"I don't think so," Vanessa said, keeping her voice down. "But I can't talk about it here."

"Do you want to leave?"

The question was music to her ears. She grabbed her purse. "Let's not stop to say hello."

Lucy nodded and rose from the table. "I wouldn't dream of it."

They slipped out the front door without Brock noticing them. He was oblivious to anything but what he wanted, when he wanted it.

He'd made love to Vanessa days ago, then kissed her with enough passion to make her toes curl and her heart ache every time they'd been together since. He'd made her doubt herself, her intentions and her life.

But she was glad she'd come here tonight.

Seeing him with another woman firmed up her resolve. Seeing him with Larissa reminded her what kind of man he really was. She'd been a fool. She wouldn't allow herself warm feelings for him. She certainly wouldn't fall in love with him now. Her course was set. She wasn't finished with Brock yet. She owed him for the pain he'd caused her sister. She had three major events coming up and the plans to disrupt each one were solidly planted in her head.

There was no turning back.

Brock would get exactly what was coming to him.

# Nine

"I want to give you what you've got coming, Vanessa," Brock said, standing behind his desk wearing a devastating smile. She'd been summoned to his office just a few minutes ago and hadn't a clue what he'd wanted.

He paced now, hands clasped behind his back. In an uncharacteristic business tone, one he almost never took with Vanessa, he began, "You've been here about six weeks now."

Vanessa nodded, estimating in her head that he was correct give or take a day.

"And in that time, you've worked hard. I've seen the hours you put in. Your efforts haven't gone unnoticed."

His sensuous mouth curled up in another smile. "I'm speaking as your employer now, Vanessa."

She gulped. What was Brock up to?

"Let me get to the point, I'm giving you a bonus."

Vanessa flinched inwardly. How had she botched up her plan so much that Brock offered up a bonus? The news crushed her, but she maintained her outward composure.

"Since you've been here, working on events, the hotel has thrived."

"Oh." More bad news.

Vanessa kept disappointment from her voice the best she could. Her last three attempted foul-ups had become hugely successful events. "I'm happy to hear that."

"I'm sure you are." Brock's tone sharpened for a second. "It's why I hired you. I knew you were the only one for the job."

She nodded with a feigned smile, swallowing a lump that lodged in the pit of her stomach. It was still a mystery to her how she'd deliberately underbooked last weekend's luau only to have the event sell out at the last minute.

The amateur Surf and Turf BBQ on the beach had gone off without a hitch, even though she'd *misplaced* the surfboards and made sure the propane tanks were empty in the gas grills. But no panic ensued. Somehow, everything had come together and the guests wound up having a marvelous time.

Even the one hundred geckos released around the

pool during the new innovative Water Massage Demonstration hadn't caused the uproar she'd hoped. Hotel security had rounded up the tiny green lizards within seconds. There'd been no scrambling, no wild screams from the guests, no chaos. In fact, the slight disturbance only proved how well the water massage worked. The guest going through the demonstration hadn't even flinched, displaying uncanny evidence how effective the relaxing technique worked.

Vanessa had failed miserably and now, adding insult to injury, Brock handed her a bonus envelope. "You deserve this more than I can say."

She gazed down at the envelope, biting her lip. "Thank you."

"You're welcome. Open it."

"No, I, uh…I'll open it later."

Goodness, she didn't want to see the monetary extent of her failure. She didn't know if she could pull off a grateful smile. Tears threatened and she banked them down.

"If that's what you want. You'll find it generous. Personal feelings aside, you've done a bang-up job here at Tempest Maui."

*Botched* was the better term. "Thank you, Brock. Anything else?"

Brock relaxed his stance and came around his desk. Leaning on the corner, he folded his arms over his chest. "How are the wedding plans going?"

She blinked. "Smoothly."

"Great. Is there anything you need from me?"

Vanessa shook her head. "Not at the moment." She'd hoped she'd have ruined him by now. Instead, she'd helped his hotel make money hand over fist. How had that happened?

Baffled, Vanessa debated about whether or not to sabotage the double wedding. It would be lower than low on her part. Brock's mother had finally found happiness after years of being a widow. But, how better to ruin the hotel's reputation if the owner's very own family wedding turned out as a nightmarish fiasco?

Her face fell at the prospect.

"Anything wrong, Vanessa?"

"What?" Vanessa peered into Brock's concerned eyes. "Oh, no." She waved the unopened bonus envelope in the air. "What could be wrong? I'm glad you're happy with my work."

Brock slanted her a look. "Thrilled is more like it. I'll probably win my bet with Trent. And I have *you* to thank for that."

Her heart sunk to her feet. "Right, the bet that your hotel will outperform his hotel in Arizona."

"Then there's the matter of winning my father's classic Thunderbird." Brock's voice quieted and he gazed deep into her eyes. "I can't wait to show you that car."

The moment Brock lifted up and approached her with a hot gleam in his eyes, Vanessa spotted trouble with a capital *T*. She backed up instantly, almost stumbling. "I'd better get back to work."

Brock pursed his lips, disappointed, but he let her go without stopping her and she made a clumsy escape. She had big decisions to make regarding the Tyler double wedding coming up next week.

Could she destroy two innocent Tyler weddings just to prove a point?

At the end of the day she walked out of her office, the Tempest envelope stuck between her checkbooks and her wallet in her purse, still unopened. She hated that it was in there, hated what it represented.

When she reached her condo, she stripped out of her clothes, ran bathwater scented with plumeria and stepped in. Warm water surrounded her weary bones and she melted into the sweetly fragranced bath until she finally relaxed.

When Plan A doesn't work, you go to Plan B, she told herself. But Vanessa didn't have another plan. Certain that her sabotage would work and she'd be free of Brock Tyler by now, Vanessa had only this one vision.

"Now what?" she whispered, cupping water over her bare shoulders and arms.

Vanessa glanced at her new Lily's Designs alligator purse she'd tossed on the bathroom counter. Not a knockoff this time. Lily herself had given the purse to her after the conference concluded for a job well done.

Another reflection of her plan gone awry.

Her muscles tightened once again. She glared at the

purse, thought of the bonus it housed inside and mentally chastised herself all over again for failing.

"Don't open it, Vanessa. Don't cash the check. Don't even think about it."

But curiosity got the better of her. She stepped out of the tub, covered herself with a big towel and walked over to her purse. Biting her lip, she snapped it open and pulled the envelope out.

On a deep breath, she ripped open the envelope and gasped when she saw the amount on the check. Tears immediately welled up. She'd made Brock a fortune and he'd given her a percentage of that for her good work.

She found a note enfolded inside the envelope. With a flick of her fingers, the note parted.

*Join me tonight on the* Rebecca *at seven sharp to celebrate.*

Vanessa stared at the note. Those commanding words just added to her dismay. Brock thought he could summon her at his will, whenever he wanted. Anger bubbled up. Her nerves grew tight. Her body shook. The implication was clear. He'd given her a large amount of money and now expected her to pay up with the one *other* thing that was important to him. Sex. She whispered, "How dare you, Brock."

Vanessa dressed quickly, putting on a seductive little gown, piled her hair up with a clip and put on her best jewelry. She wanted out. And she wanted Brock to see what he'd be missing when she told him off and walked out on him.

Vanessa reached the yacht just as the sun set on the horizon. Festive twinkling lights illuminated the marina and dock, guiding her way to Brock's boat.

She found Brock easily enough, looking handsome in tan trousers and a black silk shirt on the deck, waving her aboard. He met her when she approached and helped her climb the steps. "Glad you could make it."

She nearly snorted. "Did I have a choice?"

Brock grinned and took her hand. "I have something to show you."

"I bet you do."

He guided her down the stairs leading to the main sitting room. Suddenly, bright lights flashed, cameras went off and a roomful of people called out, "Surprise!"

Startled, Vanessa backed up a step, only to fall back against Brock's willing arms. She righted herself and looked up at the sign above the wet bar. "Vanessa Dupree—Tempest Employee of the Month."

She glanced at Lucy, who couldn't keep from grinning, Akamu and two dozen coworkers she'd come to know from the Tempest offices, all welcoming her with smiles. She turned to Brock. "Are you serious?"

He smiled, a gleam in his eyes unreadable. "Dead serious."

"You throw an elaborate party for your Employees of the Month?"

"Not every month. Just when someone exceeds our expectations."

A glass of champagne was shoved into her hand and Lucy came over to give her a hug. "Congrats. This is a great honor."

"But I…um." What could she say? "Thanks."

Brock took that opportunity to give a little speech about the hotel's recent success and Vanessa's part in that. She was met with a round of applause and afterward they dined on a catered buffet outside on the deck. The night was warm for late winter, but that didn't stop Vanessa from getting chilled to the bone.

She hadn't expected this. *None of it.* She didn't deserve the friends she'd made here. She didn't deserve to have Lucy's and Akamu's support and love, either.

The yacht toured the bay, moving slowly and Vanessa found herself alone at the railing, looking out at Tranquility Bay, fully enraptured in the moment.

A wealth of emotions sought her out: guilt, joy, loyalty, deceit, allegiance, cowardice. Her head spun with confusing thoughts. And then the "if onlys" took hold.

*If only* all of this was real, the job and the friends she'd made here.

*If only* she deserved the honors bestowed upon her for a job well done.

*If only* she was free to fall in love with Brock Tyler without guilt or deception.

When the yacht docked, Vanessa said goodbye to

all of her friends and coworkers, thanking them for coming and sharing this special time with her.

After everyone had left, Brock walked up to her, took her hand, and she gazed deep into his eyes. She'd accused him of horrible things, but he'd been up front and honest with her. More than she'd been with him.

Except, one thing bothered her and she had to know the truth. "I saw you at the Torch with Larissa Montrayne the other night."

"I was there." He nodded quietly and sipped his champagne.

"You admit it?"

"Yes. I didn't see you."

"I left."

"If you'd have stayed longer, you would have seen her fiancé come in. I met Larissa in the parking lot. I didn't take her there. She'd been waiting for him and we decided to grab a drink inside."

"That's it?"

"That's it." He leaned in and kissed her lips. He tasted of warm alcohol, smelled like musk and looked like sin itself. "Anything else?"

Had it been that simple? Had Brock met Larissa like he'd claimed? Had it been an accidental meeting? She'd only stuck around for a minute after seeing him at the Torch before thinking the worst and running off.

Vanessa connected with his eyes. Whenever he looked at her she saw desire, a mesmerizing gleam that drew her in with magnetic force. She swallowed hard and did a mental head shake.

She'd come here so determined and now she felt herself melting, losing herself in him again. "I should go," she whispered.

Brock cupped her face with one hand. "I need you tonight, Vanessa."

It wasn't a command or a demand. It was a statement of fact. The sweetly earnest tone of his voice charmed her.

"Why me, Brock?" Her question slipped out. It was a question she'd been asking herself since she arrived on the island. They'd been inexplicably drawn together and it was the last thing she'd wanted.

But here they were—a man with playboy tendencies and a woman who despised that lifestyle. She nibbled her lip. "You could have any woman—"

"That's not my style." Vanessa arched her brows, which prompted him to add, "Anymore."

Brock drew her into his strong arms. "We're wasting the night talking. I promise to answer all your questions in the morning. Stay, baby."

He took her hand and Vanessa followed him to the bedroom.

Brock loved making love to Vanessa. She was responsive and sensitive to his every touch, every caress. She liked sex and he didn't think many women really did. They'd go through the motions to please a man, but they didn't enjoy the act itself.

Vanessa enjoyed the connection, the physicality of making love. She threw caution to the wind, knew no inhibition and lost herself in the pleasure.

Just seeing her laying on his bed, her platinum tresses spread out on the pillow, waiting for him, made him crazy for her. She was as hot for him as he was for her, and that turned him on more than anything else.

Naked and fully aroused, Brock laid down next to her on the bed. He took her into his arms and made powerful, deliberate, desperate love to her like there was no tomorrow.

Because there *was* no tomorrow.

Brock was through playing games with Vanessa. She'd gotten under his skin and when she was breathless and panting beneath him, he could almost forget her deceit. But he wouldn't allow himself that luxury. She was the enemy of her own making.

Yet everything inside him wanted to forget what she'd done and who she was. He wanted her. Period.

After tomorrow she'd be out of his life for good. He'd see to it. All they had was tonight.

And Brock planned on using his time wisely.

After their first climax together, Brock rolled onto his back, his body coated with a thin sheen of perspiration from the heat they'd created. He glanced at Vanessa, whose skin glowed with the aftermath of lovemaking.

She was so beautiful. At times he thought her vulnerable and innocent. He shook his head at the ridiculous notion that Vanessa could be either.

She lifted her head from the bed and charmed him with a pretty smile. "What are you shaking your head at?"

Brock inhaled. He'd tell her half the truth. "You. You're not what I expected."

She answered quietly, tracing a finger around his mouth. "Neither are you, sweetheart."

Brock stared at her. It was the first time she'd used an endearment with him. Her tone was sweet and sincere, which destroyed him inside.

She'd tried to make a fool of him, yet Brock couldn't think past the melodic softness of her voice when she called him *sweetheart.*

"Ready for round two?" he asked, fully aroused again.

Vanessa grinned and stroked his thick erection. "Ready. But one of us is bound to get knocked out sooner or later."

Brock groaned. "Later. Much later."

She climbed on top of him and straddled his thighs. Without hesitation, she lowered herself down and he jammed his eyes shut briefly from the exquisite sensation of Vanessa taking him in and riding him with purposeful thrusts.

He held her at the beautiful arch of her back and watched her make love to him, her head thrown back, her silvery tresses flowing.

He knew when her body couldn't take another second. He felt her tighten, the constriction pulsing around him and witnessed the look of sheer tortured pleasure on her face when her body released.

Brock let her ride it out until she was sated and damp. Then he held her hips and thrust into her once, twice. It was all he'd needed, her mind-blowing climax enough of a rush to satisfy his own.

She rested against him, her breasts crushing against his chest and Brock didn't think life got any better than this.

Sex surely didn't.

He held her until she fell asleep, then he succumbed, banishing any disturbing thoughts from entering his mind.

There was a chill in the room when Vanessa woke up. She rolled over to find Brock gone from the bed. Flashes of last night entered her sleep-induced mind. They'd made love three times during the night and each time had been more thrilling, more intimate than the time before. She smiled, remembering. Her body ached from Brock's thorough lovemaking.

Vanessa knew she was a goner.

She'd fallen head over heels in love.

She nibbled on her lower lip, more confused than ever.

*What now?*

She rose and tossed on her panties and bra, then

went in search of Brock. She found him standing by the window in the main parlor looking out at the bay, sipping whiskey.

Whiskey at seven in the morning?

Bone-chilling fear swept over her. "Brock?"

He turned and his face was an unreadable mask. For a moment, when his eyes flickered over her body, she noted a quick flash of the man who'd made love to her last night. Then as quickly as it had come, it was gone.

"You like sex, don't you, Vanessa?"

"Sex?" What kind of question was that? "Yes, with the right man. Of course."

He nodded and finished the tumbler full of whiskey in one gulp. "The right man? Hell, I'd hate to see what you'd do if you were with the *wrong* man."

Confused, Vanessa shook her head several times. "What are you talking about?"

Brock slammed his glass tumbler down and she jumped. "I know who you are, Vanessa. I know how you set out to sabotage my hotel. I know everything."

Vanessa blinked. Then gasped and took a step back, suddenly feeling vulnerable in her half-naked state.

She saw a man's dinner jacket lying over the sofa and put it on, her heart racing like mad.

Brock knew? How had he found out?

Her stomach squeezed tight.

Before she could formulate her thoughts, he approached her. "Was having sex with me your way of distracting me from the truth?" he asked, his jaw tight, his lips even tighter.

She couldn't believe the accusation. "Me? You're accusing *me* of using *you* for sex?" Suddenly, Vanessa's temper flared. "That's rich, Brock. You're the one who charms innocent young girls then drops them like hot potatoes, breaking their hearts!"

Brock's face evened to a placid expression. "You're confusing me with someone else, babe."

"No, you broke my sister's heart. You hurt her badly, Brock. You didn't give a damn about it either. She told me all about how you dumped her for another woman. *Melody Applegate?* Or do you even remember her?"

"I remember her."

"So you admit it!"

"I dated her for half a minute. I don't know what she told you, but she was a sweet kid and we parted as friends."

"You nearly destroyed her! She's been crying and distraught ever since."

"Wrong. Take it up with her. As of right now, you'll have plenty of opportunity. You're fired, Vanessa. I want you off Tempest property before noon."

Vanessa gasped again. She should have expected this, but she'd never been fired before and it stung. Raw emotion racked her system, the pain twisting in her gut. "I hate you."

He shrugged. "I know. I've known it all along, even

when you were making love to me until I could barely take my next breath."

Vanessa slapped his face.

But it didn't affect him. He spoke with calm resolve. "You set out to destroy me, didn't you? How stupid did you think I was? After your first few attempts, I was on to you. Didn't you think it odd that all of your attempts failed after the first few? I have to admit, the geckos were a stroke of genius. You're entertaining, Vanessa. I'll give you that. Your level of deceit amazes me."

Vanessa's lips trembled. She'd been taken for a fool. And he'd been basking in her failures, enjoying every minute of it. The bonus and last night's party was a calculated ruse. Brock had secured his payback. He must be so proud of himself.

The ache of it went straight to her heart.

"Did you really think I'd stand by and let you ruin my mother's and brother's wedding? Every plan you've made on their behalf has been changed."

She shook uncontrollably. Tears stung her eyes. Brock obviously thought her lower than a snake. "No," she said, shaking her head. "I wouldn't do that. I couldn't."

His eyes narrowed. "And why should I believe that?"

Vanessa wanted to defend herself, to tell him she had limits. The problems she had with him didn't overlap into his family. She had nothing against them.

She couldn't bring herself to ruin a widow's new marriage, or a brother who had done nothing to her. But she feared her pleas would go on deaf ears. He had his mind made up about her.

Brock watched her discomfort, his gaze flowing over her as if memorizing her every move. "Go," he demanded, his voice filled with regret.

Vanessa didn't want to leave this way. She wanted to know the truth. What had gone on between Brock and her sister?

"Go," he repeated, his voice firm but quiet. "Before I bring you up on charges."

Shocked, a surprised gasp tumbled out. "Are you threatening to go to the police?"

"I have a right."

"You are a bastard, aren't you?"

"I protect what's mine, Vanessa."

Brock walked out of the room and onto the deck.

By the time she dressed and left the yacht, he was nowhere in sight.

Tears streamed down her face the whole time Vanessa packed up her clothes from the condo. She couldn't control her sobs as she returned the keys to the manager and only contained her crying long enough to turn in her leased MINI Cooper before she broke out in another pitiful bout of sobbing.

She didn't have the heart to face Lucy or Akamu, her new dear friends who had been so kind to her when she'd come to the island. Bolstering her nerve and momentarily quieting her tears, she'd placed voice mail messages on their cell phones—the coward's way out—to let them know that something had come up at home and she had to leave immediately. She fully planned on speaking with them personally, once she got this whole mess straightened out.

Her thoughts turned to Melody. Her sister hadn't answered her phone calls and she couldn't reach her on her cell either. "Melly, where are you?"

She sniffled, her eyes burning from crying as she rode in the cab to the airport. Her sister was an adult, but Vanessa still worried about her. "I'm on my way home," she whispered to the deaf walls of the taxi as she passed palms and sugarcane fields, leaving the ocean behind.

Vanessa watched the island become nothing more than a speck of sand from high above in the airplane. She stifled sobs, holding tissues to her nose, trying not to garner attention from the other passengers. Yet when she dared to peek around the cabin, she met with sympathetic eyes.

Melody will straighten this all out, she told herself. Yet Brock had been so convincing that he knew nothing about Melody's heartache. He'd lied to her before. He'd fooled her. Made love to her. She'd like to believe at least that part was honest. It had been for her. Making love to Brock hadn't been part of the plan, though he'd accused her of it. He'd accused her of many things and some were true. But the most important of his accusations about her were wrong. She hadn't used sex to throw him off track about her sabotage. And she wouldn't have ever compromised his family's wedding plans.

It hurt her deeply that he would think it. Yet she couldn't blame him entirely. She'd given him ample reason to believe the very worst about her.

A sob escaped and she sucked in oxygen, making noises that had passengers turning their heads.

Once she landed in New Orleans, she headed straight for Melody's apartment. Her tears gone, only a pitiful ache remained in her gut. Grateful they shared keys to each other's apartments, she turned the key in the lock and entered. Her shoulders slumped and her limbs went limp as every ounce of her body surrendered to exhaustion.

Melody jumped up from the sofa, wearing a smile beaming from ear to ear. "Vanny, what are you doing here?"

"I, uh..." Vanessa knew a moment of joy, seeing her sister looking healthy and fit, then glanced past her to the sofa to find Melody had company. She directed her attention back at her sister. "It's...a long story."

"Never mind. Tell me later." Melody's smile broadened and as her red hair caught the afternoon light, she positively glowed. "I have the best news!"

Vanessa blinked. The man sitting on the sofa stood to his full six-foot frame and sent her a sheepish smile.

She recognized him. She turned to her sister, curious. Warning bells rang out in her head. “What news?”

Melody stuck her left hand in Vanessa’s face and wiggled her fingers. “I’m engaged!”

# Ten

Vanessa stared at Melody in shock. "Excuse me. What?" It took her a full five seconds to wrap her mind around what'd she'd heard. "You're *engaged?*"

"Yes!" Melody could barely contain her joy. She bobbed up and down again like a child who'd won a big prize.

Vanessa's eye twitched. Lord, she hadn't twitched like that since she'd found her college boyfriend playing doctor with her best friend.

"You remember Ryan Gains."

Ryan stood beside Melody, wrapping an arm around her shoulder. "Hi, Vanessa. It's been a long time."

"Ryan," she said, trying to sort this out. "I remember you." Vanessa scratched her head, slanted him a look and pursed her lips. To Vanessa's knowledge, the high school football star had dated her sister briefly in their senior year. Melody had the biggest crush on him. "Didn't you marry right out of high school?"

"He's divorced now," Melody explained.

Vanessa shot Melody a stare.

"Don't look at me like that. I didn't have anything to do with the break up."

Vanessa sucked oxygen into her lungs. None of this seemed real. She felt like she'd been tossed into a nightmarish episode of the *Twilight Zone.* "Ryan, would you give me some time alone with my sister?"

Ryan glanced at Melody, then nodded. "Sure, I've got to get back to Tempest anyway." He turned to Melody. "Bye, honey." He took her into his arms and laid a thirty-second kiss on her. Melody nearly swooned watching him walk out the door.

"You didn't even congratulate us," Melody complained once she focused on Vanessa again. She flopped onto the sofa.

"Congratulate you?" Vanessa took a seat, fearful that what would come next would buckle her knees anyway. "I thought you were heartbroken! Destroyed. Devastated."

"Gosh, Vanny. You sound like you're sorry I'm not."

"Don't be ridiculous. I just want the truth. And what's this about Ryan getting back to Tempest?"

"He works there. He was promoted to hotel manager. When Brock left, the chain of command changed."

"Brock?" Vanessa's heart surged, hearing his name. "I thought you were madly in love with him. I thought Brock was the only man for you."

"Oh, that." Melody waved her off. "That was nothing."

"Nothing, you cried your heart out for days! My God, I thought you were suicidal at one point. That's all I heard from you. 'Brock destroyed me. I'll never love again. I can't go on without him.'"

Melody's gaze darted away. She avoided eye contact. Vanessa's blood ran cold. Dread coursed through her system.

"It was never about Brock," Melody confessed on a quiet whisper.

*Oh, God.*

"Explain, Melly. Look me in the eye and explain."

Melody made eye contact. "Well, you know how you're always babying me? Not that I don't love you too, Vanny, but I'm old enough now to make my own decisions."

"And mistakes."

"There, you see!" Melody nearly jumped out of her seat. "You've got no faith in me."

Vanessa's eye went on a twitching field day. She rubbed the corners of her temples to calm down. "We'll argue that point later. Go on."

"Well, I've been in love with Ryan for years. Ever since high school. I knew you'd never approve, so I kept quiet, but I've been pining away for him all these years. It's the real thing, Vanny. Trust me."

Vanessa made a grunting sound.

"I saw him every day at the hotel. We'd talk casually but when I found out he was getting a divorce, I'm sorry to say I was thrilled. I made up my mind I wasn't going to let him get away this time. I could tell he liked me. He'd come into the gift shop to browse around almost daily. We flirted for weeks. And, oh, Vanny, every day I'd pray he'd ask me out. And then one day he did. We dated for a few weeks, the *best* weeks of my life. Then he stopped asking me out."

Vanessa's heart landed in her stomach. Melody painted a far different picture than what she had originally been told. She feared where this confession would take her. And she was furious with Melody on so many levels right now, all she could do was sit back and listen as her nerves tightened under her skin.

"I was beside myself. I knew he had feelings for me. We connected. We enjoyed being with each other. I was totally in love with him and had to do something. Ryan needed a good nudge."

Vanessa closed her eyes. Oh, no. "That's where Brock came in."

"Yes, Brock was handsome and rich and a ladies' man. I thought going out with him would make Ryan jealous. You know how fast hotel gossip spreads. I was desperate, Vanny. I was seriously in love and, well, a girl has to do something crazy to get her man, doesn't she?"

Vanessa bit her lip so hard she was surprised blood didn't spurt out.

"I dated Brock for a few weeks. I was so crazy in love, and even more desperate now, because Ryan didn't react at all. He stopped coming by the shop. That's when I fell apart."

"Fell apart, like claiming your life was over? That you'd never love again." Vanessa's nerves were at the breaking point. But she had to hear it all from Melody before she allowed herself the luxury. "That he ruined you for all other men?"

Melody glanced away. "Yeah, but I felt all those things. I really did. I just couldn't admit to you that I'd pined away for a married man for seven years. I had enough on my plate and I didn't want to hear your lectures. I felt humiliated that he'd rejected me. Ryan's the one, Vanessa. A girl just knows those things."

*The way Brock is the one for you.*

Vanessa bounded up from her seat fearing that thought true. She paced the floor. "Finish, Melody. I want it all."

"Well, uh. I was devastated if you remember."

Vanessa sucked in oxygen. She'd remembered.

"Nothing worked with Ryan and I thought I'd lost him again. Forever!"

Melody was such a drama queen. Vanessa rolled her

eyes. “So what did you do to change his mind?” Then it struck her. The thought had never occurred to her before. “Are you pregnant?”

“I wish!” Then she smiled. “Someday. Ryan wants children.”

“What, then?”

“I took a good piece of advice. Thanks to Brock.”

“What on earth did he say?”

“He came to see me, to let me down gently, I think. It was a gentlemanly thing to do. We’d never…uh, you know, not even close. I broke down crying and confessed my story about Ryan. Anyway, he saw how devastated I was. He was very sweet and sympathetic. He told me to go to Ryan and tell him the truth. He told me men don’t like women who play games. That if there’s anything real there, Ryan would come around. But most importantly, a man wants a woman to be up front and honest.”

Vanessa braced her hands on the back of the sofa to steady herself. “Oh, God.”

“After weeks of crying and feeling hurt and rejected, I finally got up the courage to tell Ryan the truth. And just like Brock said, he appreciated my confession. He said he was gun-shy after the divorce. It all happened so fast between us that he needed more time so he backed off. But then, just a few days ago, he told me how much he loved me and that he wanted a life with me. And I knew everything would work out.”

Looking at Melody's dreamy expression sparked Vanessa's anger. "You lied to me."

"I know. I had to."

"No, you didn't have to! You have no idea what you've done!"

"Vanny, calm down. It all worked out."

Tears sprung from Vanessa's eyes. "No, it didn't all work out! Your lies have cost me, Melody."

Vanessa ached inside from gnawing guilt. Brock had been innocent of any wrongdoing. Her stomach squeezed tight thinking of the accusations she'd tossed at him. The pain she'd caused him. The deception and lies she'd told that she'd justified unequivocally in her mind. All of it came crashing down on her, the weight a heavy burden to bear.

She loved Brock Tyler.

And he'd threatened to have her arrested.

Vanessa looked Melody in the eyes and launched into her story, making her foolish sister listen as she poured out what was left of her heart.

If confession was good for the soul then Vanessa's soul went through a superdeluxe cleansing. She'd called Akamu first and confessed everything she'd done, explaining her motivation without defending her position. She'd been wrong and she admitted it. Surprise registered briefly when Akamu confessed he'd known of her deception, too. She supposed Brock had to have an accomplice in his retaliation.

Vanessa apologized until the words wouldn't come anymore. Akamu said he understood and that the person she should be apologizing to was Brock. Before hanging up the phone, they decided to put the past behind them. Vanessa was certain and relieved that she and Akamu would remain friends.

Next she called Lucy, explained the situation and begged her forgiveness. Lucy surprised her most of all. "You're my hero, Vanessa."

"I don't feel like a hero at all."

"Listen, you made a mistake, but your motivation was dead-on. And you had the guts to follow through on your plan. I thought I was the gutsy one!"

Vanessa allowed herself a small smile. "You are. Only you don't make a fool of yourself when you think you have *right* on your side. I went full steam ahead, but not without guilt, Lucy. I want you to know that I never meant to deceive or hurt you. I just never thought I'd make such wonderful friends on the island."

"You're still my friend, Vanessa. And that means I can tell you a thing or two. First, you need to come back here and ask for Brock's forgiveness. It's been almost a week since you left and our boss has been immersing himself in work, not speaking to anyone but Akamu. He goes out on his yacht alone every night. Which makes our lives tough, since he's pulled a few of us in to helping with the double wedding."

"It's in a few days, right?"

"No, that's been changed."

"Oh, so he meant what he said. He's basically undone everything I did for the wedding, including changing the date."

Lucy didn't acknowledge what Vanessa knew for fact. "Did you know he threatened to have me arrested?"

"He wouldn't do that. Bad for business."

"That's what Akamu said!"

Lucy chuckled. "Sorry, but it's true. Akamu has been pressuring him to hire a new event planner. We need help around here. But the boss won't consider it. He only stares out the office window and shakes his head whenever Akamu brings it up."

"I've ruined him for event planners," Vanessa said sourly. "That's all I meant to him."

"I think you meant more than that…a lot more. Do you love him?"

Vanessa nibbled on her lip.

"Do you?"

"Yes," Vanessa said finally, with no joy. Shouldn't a person have joy in their heart when they admit to falling in love? "But I'm sure he hates me. He'd never trust me again. I know I tried some awful things, but he *believed* I'd ruin his family's double wedding. There's nothing I can do to change his mind."

"Now that's *not* the determined friend I know. You're gutsy, remember? And quite determined when you need to be."

Vanessa sighed into the phone. "Not anymore. I've learned my lesson."

"You'll always have my friendship, Vanessa, but if you want to maintain hero-status in my eyes, you need to do something. You can't just give up!"

"I treasure your friendship, Lucy. But I'm not a hero. I'm furious with Melody for lying to me, yet I did the same thing to people I cared about." Vanessa's eyes misted and she held back tears. She was through crying outwardly, but inside she bled with infinite remorse. "I played a dangerous game and I lost."

The next day, Melody barged into the guest bedroom she'd offered Vanessa for the time being. She didn't have a job or a place to stay. Her own apartment five miles away was rented out until summer. "When are you gonna stop moping?"

"I'm not moping," Vanessa defended, lying sideways on the bed. "I'm job searching." She flipped the newspaper to the want ads and pretended interest.

"I've never seen you like this," Melody said.

"I've never been in this position before. Hmmm, I can't seem to find 'saboteur' in any job description."

"Cut it out, Vanny. You're scaring me. You've always been the dependable one."

Vanessa shook her head with wry amusement. "I babied you. Mothered you until I smothered you. I was furious with you a few days ago, but now I've had time to reflect. I understand why you lied to me. I probably would have lied to me."

Melody sat down on the bed. "Oh, no, Vanessa. You didn't baby me too much. I needed you. When Mom got really bad, I was still young and you were there, showing me that you cared. You have no idea how much that meant to me. You're my big half sister but you always were my whole sister in every way. I took you for granted and I realize, now that I'm older, how much you sacrificed for me. I love you so much for being exactly who you are. A sister who'd go to battle for me, when she thinks I've been wronged."

Vanessa sat up on the bed and slanted her sister a look. "Really?"

Melody nodded. "Really and truly."

"Thank you," Vanessa said quietly.

Melody reached out and took Vanessa's hand. "I've learned not to play games with people's emotions. Honesty works. And if it doesn't, then you gave it your best shot."

"Why do I think a lecture is coming?" Vanessa asked.

Melody smiled wisely. "Because you're the expert on giving them. Now it's my turn. Be still. Be quiet and listen to me."

"Gosh, now you're repeating my words."

"Heaven knows I've heard them so many times, they're ingrained in my head. Now, about Brock Tyler…"

* * *

The view from his rental house was breathtaking. Brock stood out on the backyard cliff overlooking the Pacific Ocean with a vodka tonic in one hand and a cell phone in the other. He had calls to make, business to conduct, but today he wasn't in the mood.

Instead he stared down at the blue waters cast somewhat murky by gray clouds overhead, lost in thought. He hadn't really planned on business calls when he took his phone out of his pocket. No, he'd been tempted to call Vanessa Dupree.

But he couldn't bring himself to speak to her by phone. He wasn't ready to forgive her. He might never be ready. He feared he'd fumble his words and end up arguing with her again. The anger hadn't yet faded, but something else was there, too, and that something had kept him from sleep every night since she'd left.

Vanessa had him fooled and not too many people had ever accomplished that with him. He thought he knew her. He thought, now here's a real woman, someone he wanted to know on every level. When he'd been with her, fleeting thoughts entered his mind of settling down, of caving in and abandoning bachelorhood like his brothers Evan and Trent and his best friend, Code.

Thoughts of Vanessa tormented him since he ordered her off his property. He couldn't shake her. Brock slipped his phone back in his pocket, writing off any idea of calling her, and sipped his drink. The strong liquor, more vodka than tonic, burned his throat and dulled his senses, but nothing washed Vanessa's image from his mind. She'd tried to ruin him, and yet when he compared her to the other women he'd known in his life, she always came out on top.

Hell, he was a fool and an idiot.

Because, still with all she'd done, he had to admire her loyalty to her sister. Vanessa thought Melody had been wronged and she went full steam ahead with her plan to exact her revenge. Brock understood that in an elemental way. He'd do anything for his brothers.

The clouds drew closer to shore, marring the last burst of sunlight on the horizon and putting a chill in the air. The weather matched his mood.

Stormy.

Brock polished off his drink and sought his nightly escape on the *Rebecca.* Sailing off at sunset brought him clarity, and he needed that right now. His mind rattled with unease. Was letting Vanessa go in his best interests? Everything inside him pushed and pulled. He wanted to go after her.

He missed her like hell.

"A girl has to do something crazy to get her man, doesn't she?" Vanessa repeated her sister's words in a whisper as she secretly slipped onto the *Rebecca.*

*You can't just give up.* Lucy's advice rang in her head.

If this didn't work, she'd blame both of them for planting the seeds.

Of course, if she were really brave, she'd confront Brock face-to-face in his office, or at his home. Instead, she chose to stow away on his yacht where he couldn't turn her away.

He could throw her overboard, though. The image passed in her head and she immediately discounted it. Brock wouldn't do that.

*That* would be terrible for business.

"You love him. Tell him, Vanessa," she said, sneaking into the bedroom where they'd made love. "Tell him you're sorry you misjudged him."

Vanessa took her shoes off and waited.

It had been a horrific day. She'd been taken out of the line at the airport for a security check and if that hadn't been enough, her flight had been delayed. The airplane had been kept on the runway for thirty minutes before allowing them clearance for takeoff. When they'd finally landed, she'd discovered her luggage had been lost.

Vanessa took everything in stride. She was determined to see this through and find out, once and for all, if she'd destroyed any chance she'd had for happiness with Brock.

She glanced at her watch. She was still on Louisiana time, but she figured it was past seven here, since the sun had already set and there was a chill in the air. She hadn't seen Lucy yet. She hadn't told a soul her plan. All Melody knew was that she was heading back to Maui to talk with Brock.

Vanessa shivered as she sat in the dark on the bed. She pulled up a blanket and wrapped it around herself. She closed her eyes just to rest them a little and laid her head back.

The boat swayed and stirred restlessly and Vanessa popped her eyes open, realizing they were out to sea. She must have fallen asleep.

Which meant that if they were moving, Brock was on board. Vanessa rose and almost lost her footing. The boat rocked back and forth. Rain pelted down, the sky dark and dismal from what she could see out the window.

She made her way carefully to the deck and came face-to-face with Brock, dripping wet, helping his crew stow away equipment. He took one look at her and cursed.

"Damn it, Vanessa. What the hell are you doing here?"

He didn't give her time to answer. He grabbed her arm and led her to his room. "There's a hurricane out at sea. We're getting hit with a big storm. Stay down here. I'll be back later."

With that, he left and Vanessa shivered. Not from the cold. Not from the storm they'd encountered. But by Brock's chilling tone. It was clear to her she'd made a big mistake coming here and now there was no escape. She'd have to wait out the storm and hope she'd be left with some semblance of dignity when they made it back to shore.

She ached inside, the pain the worst she'd ever felt in her life. She'd lost a really good man, and she may never recover. Brock's fierce expression told her all she needed to know. She experienced the same hollow hurt that Melody felt when Ryan had rejected her. She understood better now the devastating loss.

Waves crashed and the boat rocked violently. Vanessa's fear intensified. She'd been thrown a few times, so she laid down again, hugged the bedpost for support, closed her eyes and waited for the storm to end.

The next time Vanessa opened her eyes, she found Brock beside her, his warmth soothing her, his arm draped around her body. She blinked and thought she was dreaming.

"Hi," he said, gazing at her softly. "We're out of danger and almost back to Tranquility Bay."

Vanessa swallowed and nodded. Cushioned by his strong capable arms and looking into his seriously gorgeous face, she could think of worse disasters. "Will you have me arrested for breaking and entering?"

Brock smiled and traced the corners of her mouth with a finger. "That depends. Why are you here?"

She turned to her side to face him fully. "To ask for your forgiveness. I've misjudged you. Melody told me everything. She lied to me, Brock, and made me think awful things about you. I know that doesn't justify what I did and I don't know how to apologize enough. I'm probably the last person you want to see right—"

"Wrong," he said firmly. "When I saw you here, my heart nearly flew out of my chest. My feelings for you were cemented when you came on deck during the storm. I thought you might get hurt. Or tossed overboard. I couldn't stand anything happening to you. Not on my watch. Remember, I protect what's mine." He rose from the bed. "Wait here."

He left her cold and curious. When he returned, he held an orchid. He laid down on the bed again and placed the light purple flower behind her left ear. "Consider yourself taken, but not just for tonight this time, Vanessa. I'm in love with you."

Hope swelled in her heart. "I'm in love with you, too."

"I want you in my life forever."

"I want that, too…so much." Then Vanessa shook her head. "But I don't understand why you would."

"For sex, why else?" A mischievous gleam entered his eyes and then he kissed her deeply before she could react. "Lucy and Akamu came to me tonight. They pleaded your case but, honey, they didn't have to. You weren't the only guilty party. I played along and I'm sorry for lying to you. I was just as deceitful as you were. I could have confronted you when I first found out what you were doing, but I chose to play your game and drag it out. I hope you can forgive me."

"I do forgive you."

Brock sighed and admitted, "I booked a trip to the mainland to see you before they spoke with me. I had to know if I was crazy falling in love with a woman who would see me ruined."

"But it was a mistake! And I'm so sorry."

"How sorry?"

"Very, very sorry."

"Sorry enough to come to the double wedding with me as my fiancée?"

"Oh, yes," she answered, breathless. "I would love to."

"And no more games?" he asked softly.

"I promise, the only games I'll play from now on will be in bed with you."

Brock grinned. "I can wrap my mind around that. You know, I'll have to thank Melody next time I see her."

"You can't possibly be glad she lied about you."

"I am. If she hadn't made up that crazy story, you wouldn't have come to the island. And we wouldn't have met."

"Even after all the trouble I caused you? I was such a—"

Brock put a finger to her mouth, stopping her sentiment. "You were just what I needed—a beautiful, smart, determined *challenge.* The hardest thing I've ever done was to throw you off Tempest property. All I wanted was to love you."

Joy warmed her heart. "Really? That's sweet."

"I'm a sweet guy, when given the chance. So it's a date. You and me, forever?"

"It's a date, sweetheart," she replied, kissing him softly. "I'm crazy in love with you."

Brock relaxed against the bed and released a big sigh. "That's a relief." He nuzzled her throat and came up over her on the bed, another teasing glint entering his eyes. "A really good event planner is hard to find."

# Epilogue

"Geckos? There are geckos roaming the grounds again?"

Brock glanced around the Garden Pavilion where his mother and Matthew were speaking vows. His brother Trent and his fiancée, Julia, were standing next to them.

"Don't look at me," Vanessa whispered, innocently. "I learned my lesson."

"It's taken care of, boss," Akamu said quietly. "Willie Benton has been collecting them for a week and they got loose on the property."

"Got loose? Or were let out?" Their young hotel guest had a reputation for making mischief.

Akamu shrugged. “Don’t know. There must have been about three dozen running around. Security has them all rounded up.”

Brock nodded and glanced at his beautiful fiancée. Soon they’d be saying their vows and Brock couldn’t wait. He took her hand and together they watched the weddings take place without a hitch.

Sarah Rose, famous country singer and now his best friend, Code’s, wife sang sweet ballads throughout the ceremony, looking happily pregnant. Code stood beside her with pride.

Evan and Laney stood as best man and maid of honor, and little John Charles Tyler Junior sat in his stroller, the youngest ever Tempest Maui ring bearer.

The ceremony ended amid a round of applause from family and friends as the newly married couples made their way down the aisle.

Afterward, the Tylers got together for a brief meeting of the minds. Brock gave a toast then took Vanessa in his arms. “I’m gracefully bowing out of the competition with Trent even though I’m certain I’m the winner.”

He winked at his fiancée and joy filled his heart enough to last an eternity. No more games for him either. He considered himself a winner, just by loving Vanessa.

“Wait a minute,” Trent said, holding Julia’s hand. “You beat me to the punch, brother. I was planning on opting out of the competition.” He and Julia exchanged loving glances. "Tempest West is thriving and I'm sure *I'm* the winner, but it's not important now."

Brock squeezed Vanessa's shoulder, bringing her closer. "So I'm out and you're out."

They all turned to Evan, who held his new son with his wife Laney looking on. "You guys are no fun anymore."

Brock glanced at Trent and when he nodded, Brock stepped up. "Trent and I agree that Dad's T-Bird should go to you, Evan."

Rebecca stood with tears in her eyes, beside her new husband, Matthew. "I think that's fair."

When Evan balked, Brock went on. "For your son. He's the first Tyler heir—the beginning of a new generation. It's fitting that John Charles gets the car when he's old enough."

"Like when he's thirty," Laney said seriously and everyone laughed.

Evan peered lovingly at the son he held in his arms. "Did you hear that? You're not even one yet and you've got your first set of wheels already. Say thank-you to your uncles."

And John Charles Tyler Junior promptly cooed.

* * * * *

*Harlequin is 60 years old, and Harlequin Blaze is celebrating!*
*After all, a lot can happen in 60 years, or 60 minutes…or 60 seconds!*
*Find out what's going down in Blaze's heart-stopping new miniseries,*
FROM 0 TO 60!
*Getting from "Hello" to "How was it?" can happen fast….*

*Here's a sneak peek of the first book,*
*A LONG, HARD RIDE*
*by Alison Kent*
*Available March 2009*

"IS THAT FOR ME?" Trey asked.

Cardin Worth cocked her head to the side and considered how much better the day already seemed. "Good morning to you, too."

When she didn't hold out the second cup of coffee for him to take, he came closer. She sipped from her heavy white mug, hiding her grin and her giddy rush of nerves behind it.

But when he stopped in front of her, she made the mistake of lowering her gaze from his face to the exposed strip of his chest. It was either give him his cup of coffee or bury her nose against him and breathe in. She remembered so clearly how he smelled. How he tasted.

She gave him his coffee.

After taking a quick gulp, he smiled and said, "Good morning, Cardin. I hope the floor wasn't too hard for you."

The hardness of the floor hadn't been the problem. She shook her head. "Are you kidding? I slept like a baby, swaddled in my sleeping bag."

"In my sleeping bag, you mean."

If he wanted to get technical, yeah. "Thanks for the loaner. It made sleeping on the floor almost bearable." As had the warmth of his spooned body, she thought, then quickly changed the subject. "I saw you have a loaf of bread and some eggs. Would you like me to cook breakfast?"

He lowered his coffee mug slowly, his gaze as warm as the sun on her shoulders, as the ceramic heating her hands. "I didn't bring you out here to wait on me."

"You didn't bring me out here at all. I volunteered to come."

"To help me get ready for the race. Not to serve me."

"It's just breakfast, Trey. And coffee." Even if last night it had been more. Even if the way he was looking at her made her want to climb back into that sleeping bag. "I work much better when my stomach's not growling. I thought it might be the same for you."

"It is, but I'll cook. You made the coffee."

"That's because I can't work at all without caffeine."

"If I'd known that, I would've put on a pot as soon as I got up."

"What time *did* you get up?" Judging by the sun's position, she swore it couldn't be any later than seven now. And, yeah, they'd agreed to start working at six.

"Maybe four?" he guessed, giving her a lazy smile.

"But it was almost two…" She let the sentence

dangle, finishing the thought privately. She was quite sure he knew exactly what time they'd finally fallen asleep after he'd made love to her.

The question facing her now was where did this relationship—if you could even call it *that*—go from here?

* * * * *

# COMING NEXT MONTH

## Available March 10, 2009

**#1927 THE MORETTI HEIR—Katherine Garbera**
*Man of the Month*
The one woman who can break his family's curse proposes a contract: she'll have his baby, but love must *not* be part of the bargain.

**#1928 TALL, DARK...WESTMORELAND!—Brenda Jackson**
*The Westmorelands*
Surprised when he discovers his secret lover's true identity, this Westmoreland will stop at nothing to get her back into his bed!

**#1929 TRANSFORMED INTO THE FRENCHMAN'S MISTRESS—Barbara Dunlop**
*The Hudsons of Beverly Hills*
She needs a favor, and he's determined to use that to his advantage. He'll give her what she wants *if* she agrees to his request and stays under his roof.

**#1930 SECRET BABY, PUBLIC AFFAIR—Yvonne Lindsay**
*Rogue Diamonds*
Their affair was front-page news, yet her pregnancy was still top secret. When he's called home to Tuscany and demands she join him, will passion turn to love?

**#1931 IN THE ARGENTINE'S BED—Jennifer Lewis**
*The Hardcastle Progeny*
He'll give her his DNA in exchange for a night in his bed. But even the simplest plans can lead to the biggest surprises....

**#1932 FRIDAY NIGHT MISTRESS—Jan Colley**
Publicly they were fierce enemies, yet in private, their steamy affair was all that he craved. Could their relationship evolve into something beyond their Friday night trysts?

SDCNMBPA0209